A sliding panel rolled back and we peered through a thick crystal wall at a member of the Mirt Korp Ahm.

I tried to comprehend the nature of a race whose last baby had been born in the epoch of the subhuman man-apes, whose last death had occurred in the time of the cave painters.

In the cavernous six-sided room a cluster of massive machinery converged on a cup-shaped couch of glossy blue metal. Enthroned on the couch sat a being of great size, perhaps twice the size of a human, dome-headed, four-armed, covered with scales.

Life-support mechanisms surrounded and practically engulfed it. A dozen small cubical structures were fastened to its limbs; a complex device was strapped about its chest; wires ran from its skull, its body, its wrists. This entire immense room was a nest of equipment that served to sustain the flicker of life in this creature, to nourish it and keep its organs pumping and drain off the poisons of age.

For this High One was old.
Hideously, frighteningly old.

ACROSS A BILLION YEARS

BY
ROBERT SILVERBERG

A JIM BÆN PRESENTATION:

A TOM DOHERTY ASSOCIATES BOOK

Copyright © 1969 by Robert Silverberg

A TOR Book

Published by:

Tom Doherty Associates, Inc.
8-10 West 36th Street
New York, New York 10018

First TOR printing, December 1983

ISBN: 812-55-450-7

Can. Ed.: 812-55-451-5

Cover art by Dell Harris

Printed in the United States of America

Distributed by:

Pinnacle Books, Inc.
1430 Broadway
New York, New York 10018

ACROSS A BILLION YEARS

one

Lorie, I can't even guess when you'll get to hear this letter. If ever. I mean, I might just decide to blank the message cube when I finish talking into it. Or maybe I'll forget about giving it to you when I come home from all this.

It isn't just that I'm an unstable sort of vidj, which of course I am. By the time I'm able to get any letters into your hands, though, a couple of years will have gone by, and what I have to tell you now may not seem very important or interesting. But I have these message cubes anyway. And right now it seems like a good idea to put it all down for you, to make a record of what I'm doing and what's happening to me out here.

I guess the proper thing to do tonight is to call you up on the galaxy-wide telepath hookup and wish us a happy birthday, we being twenty-two years of age this day. (Doesn't that sound ancient? We're turning into fossils!) A guy really ought to keep in touch with his twin sister on their birthday, even if she's home on Earth and he's bimpty-bump light-years away.

But it costs about a billion credits to make a live real-time skull-to-skull call. Well, maybe not that much; but whatever it costs, it's more stash than I've got in my thumb account. And I don't dare call collect, even though Our Lord And Master wouldn't suffer much from the charge. Considering the way things were between Dad and me when I took off on this jaunt, I just don't have the slice to try it. He'd split a wavelength when he saw the bill.

Will this do, then?—Happy Birthday, Sister Mine, from your unique and irreplaceable brother Tom, far, far away. I send you, via message cube and a couple of years after the fact, a chaste and brotherly kiss.

Exactly where I am now is anybody's guess. We are supposed to land on Higby V in three Earth-standard-time days, and Higby V is—what? sixty, eighty, ninety light-years from Earth?—but as you may know there isn't any one-to-one correlation between time spent in ultradrive travel and distance covered. On a journey of ten light-years, say, the ship can spend two months going a quarter of the distance, then cover the rest of the way in an hour and a half. It has something to do with the space-time manifold, and when they explained it to us laymen we were urged to visualize a needle plunging through a bunched-up sheet and sometimes going through a lot of layers at once. Higher physics of this sort has never been my pocket, exactly, and I'm not going to try to load my mind with it now. The more useless stuff from other sciences that

I attempt to learn, the more archaeology I'm going to forget, and the archaeology is more important.

It's like Professor Steuben, the Assyriologist, used to say. All semester long he called me Mr. Barley, which I thought was his idea of a joke, until I found out he really believed that that was my name. So I said my name was Rice, and the next day he called me Mr. Oats. I said my name was Rice, again. He drew himself up to about three meters high and said, "Mr. Rice, do you realize that every time I memorize one student's name, I forget one irregular verb? One must establish priorities!" He went back to calling me Barley, but he gave me an A, so I won't crank about him too much.

Professor Steuben ought to see me now, about to dig in at the galaxy's top archaeological site. I feel like the curtain's going up for me at last. You remember how we used to talk about how growing up is a kind of overture, and then Act One starts when you're out on your own? So here I am standing in the wings, listening to the last chords of the overture, hoping I don't muff my lines when the big moment comes.

Not that I mean to boost my own heat. I know and you know and we all know that I'm a very minor part of this expedition, that I'm going to get out of it more than I can possibly give to it, that I'm lucky to be here and no great asset to the enterprise. Does that fulfill my Modesty Quota for the epoch? But I mean it. I am humble on this jog, because I know I have a great deal to be humble about.

I'll feed you the data on the voyage so far first, and then I'll scan you the cast of characters as I read it up to here.

Voyage so far: zero. I wish I could paint you a thrill-

ing vivid picture of an ultradrive voyage, Lorie, to add
to your collection of vicarious experiences. Blot that,
but completely. The fact that you will never travel by
ultradrive is absolutely no cause for regret. The ship
has no windows, no scanner plates, no viewscreens, no
access to the outside environment whatever. There is
no sensation of motion. The temperature never varies,
the lights don't flicker, it rains not in here, neither
does it snow. What this trip is like is like spending a
couple of months inside one very long and low hotel
that is locked up tight in every way. Outside us, they
tell me, is a gray, featureless murk that doesn't change
at all, ever. Ultraspace is a universe having a foggy day
as long as infinity. Therefore the ship designers don't
risk structural weakness by putting in windows. The
only excitement of the voyage came on the third day,
when we were just outside the orbit of Mars and making the shift from ordinary space into ultraspace. For
about thirty seconds I felt as if someone had stuck a
hand down my gullet and pulled me inside out in one
swift yank. This is not exactly a delightful sensation.
But it's a measure of how boring things have been
since then that I'm looking forward eagerly to feeling
it again when we phase out of ultradrive tomorrow or
the next day. I guess it'll be the reverse: like getting
undisemboweled.

.   .   .

That long dumb silent place on the message cube is
where I stopped talking for a while, Lorie, while I
debated whether to go back and erase what I just said.
I mean, the part about the voyage being so dull be-

cause we can't see anything or do anything or escape from captivity.

It's a bit cloddish for me to crank about that to *you*. It holds me up all spoiled and petulant, with my miserable few months stuck in the same place, compared with what you've had to put up with for practically your whole life. All right, so I'm a clod. I don't know how you manage it, Lorie, except maybe being a telepath helps to get your mind off things. I'd have gone crazy in your place long before I was housebroken.

Still, you are you and I am I, and please make allowances for my faults, which are maximum. I don't have your saintly patience, and I'm quietly going crazy in this ship, and feel free to scorn me for having such a low tolerance for boredom.

I'll leave all of this on the cube. I want to give you the whole picture, everything I'm feeling, and devil take trying to look like a noble soul. I couldn't fool you anyway.

      .   .   .

Now for the cast of characters. And I do mean characters.

There are eleven archaeologists on this trip. Three of us are apprentices, newly outslipped from college, and archaeologists more by courtesy than by merit. On the other hand, our three bosses are utter tops in the line, each one of them deemed a major authority on the High Ones, and naturally they hate each other to a high-frequency zing. The remaining five are medium sorts, all pros but nothing special, the kind of hacks you find in any operation. They've been around, they know their stuff, they do what they're told. But they don't have much spark.

As you might expect we're a racially mixed outfit. The liberals *must* have their way. And so the quota system has been imposed on us: we include six Earthmen, counting one android, and five selected representatives of five of the other intelligent galactic races. Now, you know I'm no bigot, Lorie. I don't care how many eyes, tentacles, eating orifices, or antennae an organism happens to have, so long as it knows its stuff. What I object to is having someone who is professionally inferior jacked into an expedition simply for the sake of racial balance.

Take our android, for example. Her name is Kelly Watchman, and her specialty is vacuum-core excavation.

Kelly is probably about ninety years old, judging by her vat number, which is someplace around fifteen thousand. (They're up over a million now, aren't they?) But, being an android, she doesn't age at all, and so she looks about nineteen. A very sexy nineteen, naturally; if you're going to make artificial human beings, you might as well make good-looking ones, the android companies say, and I quite agree. Kelly is highly decorative, and goes around the ship wearing next to nothing at all, or sometimes less. Since an android doesn't have any more sex life than the Venus de Milo, Kelly doesn't stop to consider the effect that all those jiggles and curves might have on normal human males who keep bumping into her in corridors. Not me, incidentally: the first day Kelly stripped down

I noticed that she doesn't have a navel, and that turned me off thinking of her as a real woman. I mean, there's no reason why an android *ought* to have a navel, but even so I can't help visualizing her as a kind of rubber doll that walks, and I don't have any romantic interest in walking rubber dolls no matter how lifelike and voluptuous they may be. Some of the others, though—

Well, I'm off the track, and maybe my prejudices are showing a little, since a lot of people do find androids desirable. The important thing is that Kelly Watchman is aboard this ship because she's a member of a downtrodden minority, not because she's an outstanding vacuum-corer operator.

She *can't* be an outstanding vacuum-corer operator. It's well known that the android nervous system, clever as it is, doesn't match up with that of a real human. The android just doesn't have that extra sense, that ability to know that if he digs another tenth of a millimeter he'll damage some valuable artifact. An android is always 100 percent efficient at any skill he learns; the trouble is that humans, unpredictable as we are, can come through with 105 percent efficiency when the situation demands it. Maybe we aren't as cool and mechanically perfect as androids, but when the protons are popping we can rise above ourselves for brief periods of superhuman performance, and androids simply aren't programmed to do that. By definition, there can't be any android geniuses. The vacuum-corer operator on an archaeological dig *needs* to be a genius. I admire Kelly for having won her emancipation and all that, and for picking up a difficult skill, and for devoting herself to something as abstract as archaeology. All the same, I wish we had a flesh-and-blood vacuum-corer man on this dig, and I don't think that's just my bigotry coming out.

Our other digger is also part of our racial quota, but I don't feel quite the same way about him. His name is Mirrik, which is a contraction of a label as long as my arm, and he's from Dinamon IX. He's our bulldozer.

Mirrik's kind come big. Have you ever seen pictures of the extinct Earthly mammal called the rhinoceros? It was about the size of a big pickup truck—I'm sure you've seen trucks in your hookups with other telepaths—and twice as heavy. Mirrik is almost as big as a rhinoceros. He's higher at the shoulders than I am tall, and a lot longer than he is high, and he weighs and eats as much as the rest of us put together. He also smells rather ripe. His skin is blue and wrinkled, his eyes are small, and he has long flat tusks in his lower jaw. But he's intelligent, sophisticated, speaks Anglic with no accent at all, can name the American presidents or the Sumerian kings or anybody else out of Earthside history, and recites love poetry in a kind of throbbing, cooing voice. He's a pretty fantastic sort of vidj, and on top of all this he knows archaeological technique like a star, and he can lift loads that would rupture a tractor. He's going to do our heavy digging, before Kelly gets in there with her vacuum-corer, and I think it's terrific to be able to combine an archaeologist and a heavy-duty machine in the same body. He digs with his tusks, mostly, but he's got a pair of extra limbs to help out, aside from the four pillars he stands on. I like him. You have to watch out around him, though. Most of the time he's awfully gentle, but he goes on flower-eating jags and gets drunk and wild. A dozen geraniums tank him up like a liter of rum. We have this hydroponic garden on top deck, and once a week or so Mirrik gets homesick and goes up there and nibbles blossoms, and then he starts carousing through the ship. Last Tuesday he almost smeared Dr. Horkkk into a puddle on the wall.

Dr. Horkkk is one of our three bosses. He comes from Thhh, which is a planet in the Rigel system, and he's the galaxy's leading expert on the language of the High Ones. That isn't saying much, considering we can't understand a syllable of their language, but Dr. Horkkk knows more than anyone else.

I like to think of him as a German. He reminds me of the nutty therapist who used to commute from Düsseldorf every Wednesday to try to teach you to walk. Dr. Schatz, remember? Dr. Horkkk is just like him in an alien way. He's very small, very fussy, very precise, very solemn, and *very* sure of himself. Also he seems to spit when he talks. Underneath it all I think he's kindhearted, but you can't really tell, because he works so hard at being ferocious on the outside. He comes up to just about hip-high on me, and when he stands sideways you can hardly see him, he's so skinny. He's got three big bulging eyes on top of his head, and two mouths under that, one for talking and one for eating, and his brain is where his belly ought to be, and where he keeps his digestive tract I wouldn't even like to guess. He has four arms and four legs, all of them about two fingers thick, so he looks sort of spidery. When Mirrik came blundering along and almost squashed him the other day, Dr. Horkkk went straight up the wall, which was pretty scary to behold. Afterward he cranked Mirrik over in a dozen different languages, or maybe three dozen, calling him "drunken ox" in all three dozen. But Mirrik apologized and they're good friends again.

No matter what his race was, Dr. Horkkk would belong on this trip. But Steen Steen is here purely on the minority thing. I hardly need to tell you: Steen's a Calamorian, a real militant one, as if there's any other kind. He/she is one of the other apprentices, slipped last year from a Calamorian university, which must be even more of a diploma mill than rumor has it. This one doesn't know a thing. Casual discussion reveals that Steen's knowledge of the theory of archaeology is about as deep as my knowledge of the theory of neutrinics, and I don't know *anything* about neutrinics. But I don't pretend I do; and Steen is supposed to be a graduate student in archaeology. You know how he/she got here, of course. Calamorians are forever yelling about status, and threatening to make war on everybody in sight if their intellectual attainments aren't universally recognized and admired. So we're stuck with Steen by way of keeping his/her people cool.

At least Steen's good-looking: sleek and graceful, with shiny emerald skin and long twining tentacles. Every movement is like something out of a ballet. Nobody admires Steen more than Steen, but I guess that's forgivable, considering that Calamorians have both sexes in the same body and would go crazy if they didn't love themselves. But Steen is dumb, and Steen is excess baggage here, and I resent his/her presence.

The third apprentice isn't up to much either. She's a

blonde named Jan Mortenson, with a B.S. from Stock-holm University, with a cute figure and lots of big white teeth. She seems friendly but not very bright. Her father's somebody big at Galaxy Central, which is probably how she got into the expedition—these diplo-mats are always pulling rank on deals like this. I haven't had a whole lot to do with her, though: she's got her eye on our chronology man, Saul Shahmoon.

Saul doesn't have his eye on *her,* but that's her prob-lem. I don't think he's very interested in girls. He's about forty, comes from Beirut, has been working for the last five or six years at Fentnor U. on Venus. Small, dark, intense, single, reputation for good but unin-spired work. His big passion in life is collecting stamps. He brought his collection along and it fills up his whole cabin, album after album, going right back to the nineteenth century. He's had us all in there to look at it. Remember when we were saving stamps? Saul's got the things we just used to daydream about, the Marsport five-credit with the ultraviolet overprint, the Luna City souvenir sheet perforate and imperforate, the Henry XII coronation set—everything. And all the galactic stamps, stuff from fifty or a hundred planets. Jan's with him half the time, listening to his lectures on the postal system of Betelgeuse V, or wherever, or helping him get Denebian stamps off their envelopes with acid, and Saul goes on and on and on and never catches a hint. Poor Jan!

Next we have Leroy Chang, who is Associate Pro-fessor of Paleoarchaeology at Harvard, and who is very much interested in Jan, or Kelly, or anything else fe-male. I think Leroy would try to make time with Steen

Steen if he got hard up enough. Or Mirrik. Leroy says
he's Chinese, but of course his genes are as mixed up as
anyone else's from Earth, and he doesn't look any more
Chinese than I do; he's got red hair and sort of maroon
skin and a deep voice, and would probably have much
success with women if he didn't come on looking so
frantically *eager*. You don't have to be right out of
adolescence to be foolish about that sort of thing, as
Leroy proves; he's in his forties and still goopy. Professionally he's so-so, I understand. Why this expedition is so full of duds, I can't imagine.

Our Number One boss is no dud. He's Dr. Milton
Schein of Marsport University, and as you probably
are aware he's the man who excavated the first site of
High Ones artifacts near Syrtis Major. That makes him
the original paleoarchaeologist—the first man doing
anything in billion-year-old sites—and since he practically invented the science, it's hard to find fault with
him. He's superb, though a little frightening when he
begins to talk shop. In person he's a sweet warm silver-
haired type, very lovable except when his professional
jealousies start to show. He loathes Dr. Horkkk, and
vice versa, I gather because they both have such high
reputations in the field. They equally detest our third
boss, who is Pilazinool of Shilamak, the big expert on
intuitive analysis. Which means the science of jumping
to conclusions. He's good at it.

The Shilamakka, you know, have this thing about
turning themselves into machines limb by limb and
organ by organ. They start off looking surprisingly
humanoid; that is, the right number of heads, legs,
arms, and such things. I understand they have different

arrangements of joints, more fingers, fewer toes, and a couple likesuch variosities. But then they start tinkering with the basic model. A Shilamakka regards himself as zero if he doesn't have at least one artificial limb by the time he gets into adolescence. A puberty rite, sort of. And on they go through life, lopping off limbs and putting pretty metal things in their places. The less of the basic you that's left, the higher caste you are. Pilazinool is a top-rung Shilamakka, prestige maximum, and it's my guess that he's a 90 percent transplant, with not much more than his brain still organic. New heart, new lungs, new digestive system, new endocrines, new everything. A walking talking machine-man. He spends a lot of time polishing himself. He worries a lot about getting dust in his gears. I would too, I guess. When he's nervous or just thinking very hard, he's got this habit of unfastening a hand or an arm or something and playing with it. Last night in the lounge he was playing polyvalent chess with Dr. Horkkk and in one of the exciting parts Pilazinool unhitched both his legs, his left-hand audio receptor, and his right shoulder. There was this big heap of cast-off Shilamakka parts next to him. Dr. Horkkk had him in double check with a flying rook coming in strong from the side, but Pilazinool got out of it very nicely by levitating his rear right bishop, knighting two pawns, and bringing down his chief justice in one of the sweetest counterpoise moves I've ever seen. The game ended in a draw. Pilazinool is like that: chilly, more machine than man, but resourceful.

The last member of our gang is 408b of 1. I'm sorry: that's his name, or hers, or its. It comes from Bellatrix

XIV, where the fashion is to call everything by numbers. "408b" is family and personal designation. "1" is the name of the planet; they've got the whole universe numbered, and naturally their own world is Number One. Old 408b is a yellowish-looking vidj with a basically octopoid appearance, round baggy body, five walking tentacles, five grasping tentacles, a row of eyes going all the way around, and a kind of parrot-beak mouth. Its specialty is paleotechnology, and it knows a good deal about the machinery of the High Ones, though so far it hasn't imparted much of that to us. Unlike the rest of us, it isn't happy in an oxygen-nitrogen atmosphere, though it breathes it most of the time; three hours each day it goes off into a breathing chamber for a snootful of straight carbon dioxide. Mirrik thinks that 408b must be in symbiosis with some sort of plant life. Maybe so.

.   .   .

On playing this cube back, I'm unhappy about the way I seem to be putting everybody down. After all, I haven't really seen these people in action yet. I'm going by secondhand report, first impressions, and general cattiness. Maybe this is a top-level archaeological team, or will be when it gets into the field. We'll see. I don't know why I'm so sour tonight, unless I'm just getting shiny synapses from being penned up in this ship so long.

Three days more and the curtain goes up. I can't wait.

Happy birthday again, Lorie. To you. To me. To us.

two

We are here.

We did our flip-flop from ultradrive to ordinary drive right on schedule, but it wasn't as interesting as the squirmy business of going in the other direction; and then we went into orbit around Higby V and made a ho-hum landing. And got out fast, and went a little chimpo with joy at emerging from captivity.

It was a wild scene. Higby V doesn't have a real spaceport, just a big bleak empty stretch of land with some buildings at one end of it, and we came pouring out of the ship and went capering around without having to worry about port regulations. Mirrik ran up and down the field, bellowing and stamping his feet, and I did a crazy kind of dance with Jan Mortenson, and Steen Steen danced all by him/herself, and Dr. Horkkk forgot his dignity and climbed a tree, and so on. Even Kelly Watchman, who as an android doesn't suffer from a wound-up nervous system, looked relieved to be off that ship. Meanwhile the crewmen stood around tapping their skulls at us and otherwise indicating their scorn for the cargo of chimpo vidjes that they had just finished hauling across ultraspace. I can't blame them. We must have seemed pretty weird.

Then we got settled in.

Higby V is not a homey, cheering place. Maybe it was, a billion years ago when the High Ones had their outpost here. But, like Mars, which also has gone downhill a bit since the time of the High Ones, Higby V is something less than an ideal resort world today. It's about the size of Earth, but it has the mass of a Mercury-sized planet, which means low density, low gravity. No heavy elements at all. The atmosphere bled off into space a long time ago, and the oceans evaporated and did the same. There are four continents, with huge basins that once were oceans separating them. During the long spell when the planet had no air, it got a busy bombardment of meteors and other space debris, and so there are craters everywhere, same as on Mars.

A terraforming crew was here seventy years back. They planted atmosphere-generators, and by now there's a decent quantity of air, a little thin, but enough to support life. Unfortunately that causes a wind, which Higby V didn't have previously, and the wind comes sweeping across those barren plains like a knife, scooping up the sand and swirling it around. Plant life is gradually taking hold and will keep the sand down, but not for a while. The current project here is to create a self-sustaining water supply by setting up a standard evaporation-condensation-precipitation cycle, and all along the horizon you can see the hydrolysis pylons turning gas into water day and night. The immediate effect of this is to produce one miserable downpour every five or six hours.

I shouldn't crank too much however. If it weren't for the erosion that all this rain and wind has caused lately, the High Ones site would never have been uncovered.

I can imagine a more congenial place to do archaeological field work, though. The temperature here hovers just above freezing all the time; the sky is never anything but gray; the sun is an old and tired one, and doesn't break through the clouds very often; and there are no cities here, no settlements more elaborate than pioneer squatments, no recreation facilities, nothing. You have to be Dedicated to enjoy it out here.

"What use is this planet to anybody?" Jan Mortenson wanted to know. "Why did they bother terraforming it?"

Steen Steen suggested it might have radioactives. Mirrik squashed that stupid idea, pointing out that there were no metals heavier than tin here, and not much even of the lighter ones. Pilazinool believed the place had some strategic importance, maybe as a refueling stop or a monitoring station for the more valuable worlds in the next system over. But Leroy Chang, who has your true Harvard man's knack for being anti-Earth wherever possible, blurted his own explanation for why we had converted this planet to a place fit for Earthmen: politics and greed. We grabbed it, he said, to keep anybody else from having it. Pure and simple imperialism. Dumb imperialism, too, since we've spent a couple billion credits a year since the turn of the century to maintain and develop a place that has no natural resources, no tourist potential, and no other intrinsic value.

Dr. Schein challenged this interpretation, and off everybody went on a political discussion. Except me. That's one pocket I refuse to climb into.

While this was going on, Mirrik got bored and wandered away, and began digging up the turf just to have something to do. He tusked up a couple of tons of dirt in a restless way, stopped, peered into the hole he had made, and let out a booming yell. You'd have thought he accidentally had uncovered a cache of High Ones artifacts.

Well, he hadn't. But he *had* found a burial ground of Higby V natives. Maybe eighty centimeters down, the extinct inhabitants of this planet had parked about a dozen specimens, complete with weapon points, bone necklaces, and long strings of what looked like teeth. The skeletons were short and squat, with huge hind legs and little grasping paws on top.

"Cover it up," Dr. Schein ordered.

Mirrik protested. Since we were waiting around anyway for the military escort that was supposed to convoy us to our real work site, he wanted to amuse himself by digging this stuff. Saul Shahmoon was curious about it too. But Dr. Schein rightly pointed out that we had come here to excavate High Ones artifacts, not to fission around with the remains of minor local civilizations. We had no business disturbing this site; it would be a kind of vandalism if we did, since it right-fully belongs to archaeologists who are specialists in the Higby V native race. If there aren't any such specialists now, there will be someday. Mirrik saw the logic of that and carefully backfilled what he had un-earthed.

Score one for Dr. Schein. I admire professionalism.

At last our military escort arrived and transported us from the landing area to the collection of bubbleshacks that passes for Higby V's greatest metropolis. There we had a vastness of triviations to take care of. Dr. Schein handled the job of making sure our funds had been transferred into a local account, so we'd be able to get food and supplies at the base PX. Such financial details are supposed to be handled automatically by Galaxy Central, but nobody with a proper reverence for stash ever assumes that Galaxy Central gets anything straight, which is why Dr. Schein checked. Checking involved plugging into the telepath hookup. The TP on duty was a surly vidj named Marge Hotchkiss, and if you ever hook horns with her in the course of your daily work, Lorie, give her a nasty overload for me, will you? This Hotchkiss person was plump and plain, with piggy little gray eyes and a very visible mustache. About thirty-five, I guess. Except for her TP powers she is probably an extraordinarily ordinary person, the kind normally destined for a life of quiet spinsterhood in some decayed rooming house; but out here she's one of about fifty women on a planet populated by several thousand men, and that has made her arrogant beyond her station. When Dr. Schein asked her to make the hookup, she gave him a slicy smirk and insisted on his thumbprint first. He explained that he wasn't drawing on his thumb account to make the call, that he was merely requisitioning credit information from Galaxy Central and didn't have to pay. She wanted his thumb on record anyway. So he gave her the print, and then she took her sweet time about making the linkup. "Lots of interference on the line," she told us.

Completely phony, that's sure. The thing about telepathy that makes it the only practical means of interstellar communication, of course, is that there *isn't* any interference, no static, no relativistic time-lag, none of the headaches and slowdowns you get in a normal communications channel. (Blot that "normal"! What I mean, of course, is "mechanical.") All that Marge Hotchkiss had to do was reach out, grab the next TP in the relay chain, and send our message heading at instantaneous propagation toward Galaxy Central. It was her pleasure to stall, though. Finally she put the message through, and confirmed that the credit balance transfer had been made.

Dr. Schein, Dr. Horkkk, and Pilazinool went off to register their thumbprints, or equivalent identifications, so they could draw against the account here. Saul Shahmoon was given the job of picking up our excavation permit from the base headquarters. The rest of us had nothing much to do for a while, and I started to make talk with the Hotchkiss creature.

"My sister's in the TP network," I said.

"Oh."

"Her name's Lorie Rice. She works out of Earth."

"Oh."

"I thought maybe you knew her. You TP people

generally make contact with each other all over the place. Sooner or later you must come in touch with everyone else in the whole communications net."

"I don't know her."

"Lorie Rice," I said. "She's very interesting; I have to say so. I mean, she has this wonderful curiosity about the whole universe, she wants to know everything about everything. That's because she's bedridden, she can't get around anywhere much, and so the TP net sort of serves as eyes and ears for her. She gets to see the whole universe through other people's eyes, via telepathy. And if you'd ever had any contact with her, you'd remember it, because—"

"Look, I'm busy. Go get sposhed."

"Is *that* friendly? I'm just trying to make a little talk. You know, I miss my sister a whole lot, and it doesn't cost you anything if I ask you if you've ever talked to her. I—"

She brushed me off by rolling her eyeballs up into her head so that only the whites showed. It was her cute way of announcing that she was going into another TP linkup.

"Cut yourself on your own slice," I muttered, and turned away.

Jan Mortenson had been standing beside me. Now she said, "I didn't realize your sister was a TP communicator. How exciting that must be!"

"Especially for someone like her," I said. I told Jan about you being paralyzed and forced to spend your whole life in a hospital bed. Jan was very sympathetic. She wanted to know why they couldn't work some kind of Shilamakka-style transplant to put you in a synthetic body that would let you get around. This is the obvious question that everybody asks, and I explained how we investigated that a long time ago and found it was too dangerous to try in your case.

"How long has she been like this?" Jan asked.

"Since she was born. At first they thought they could correct it surgically, but—"

Then she wanted to know how old you were, and I said you were my twin, and Jan turned a very radioactive shade of scarlet and said, "If she's a TP, and you're her twin, then you must be a TP too, and you must be reading my mind *right this minute!*"

So I had to spell it all out: that we're fraternal twins and not identical twins, obviously, since you're a girl and I'm not, and that telepathy isn't necessarily shared by fraternal twin pairs, and that as a matter of fact you're the only TP in the family. I added that it's a common error to believe that a TP can read the mind of a non-TP. "They can make contact only with other TP-positive minds," I said. "Lorie can't read me. And I can't read you, or anybody else, but Fat Marge over there can read Lorie if she wants to."

"How sad for your sister," Jan said. "To have a twin brother and not to be able to reach him with TP. Especially when she's shut in and has such a need to know what's happening outside her room."

"She's a brave girl," I said, which is true. "She copes. Besides, she doesn't need me. She's got thousands of TP pals all over the universe. She spends eight hours a day hooked into the commercial telepathic communications link, relaying messages, and then I think she spends the other sixteen hours hooked in just for fun, getting TP gossip from all over. If she ever sleeps I never saw her at it. Life gave her a raw deal, sure, but she has some compensations."

Jan was very deeply interested in hearing all about you, and I told her a lot more. Which I don't need to repeat here, since you know all of it anyway. I think I may have underestimated Jan slightly. In the past few days I've started to see that her beautiful-but-dim act is only a superficial habit; she's actually a lot more sensitive and interesting than she seems. I don't know where I got this idiot notion that pretty girls are always shallow. Not that she's any blazing genius, but there's more to her than curves and a ten-kilowatt smile.

At this point most of our miscellaneous registration and checking-in had been accomplished. But we stood around for half an hour more waiting for Saul Shahmoon to get back with our excavation permit. Dr. Schein couldn't understand what was taking so long. He was afraid that Saul had run into some kind of bureaucratic roadblock that might prevent us from working on this planet altogether. That got Pilazinool so upset that he unscrewed his left arm up to the second elbow.

At last Saul came back. With the excavation permit. Seems he hadn't had any trouble about that. He had spent forty-five minutes at the PX post office, though, getting a set of Higby V stamps for his collection.

We loaded our gear into a landcrawler and off we went.

Night was falling, fast and hard. Higby V doesn't have any moons, and it's the sort of planet where, if you're close to the equator, as we are, night comes on like a switch was thrown. Zit! and it's dark. Our driver managed to keep us from going into any craters, though, and in an hour we were at the site.

Dr. Schein, who had been here last year when the discovery was made, had arranged for three bubbleshacks to be blown, one as a laboratory and two for dormitories. In addition a big curving shield of plastic covered the hillside outcropping where the High Ones artifacts had been spotted.

A complex moral thing developed when it came time to assign us to dorm space. I think you'll enjoy mulling it over.

The problem started from the fact that there are no partitions, and hence no privacy, inside the bubbleshacks. We have two unmarried Earthborn females among us, and according to the old silly tribal taboos it would be immoral and improper to let Jan and Kelly bunk with the boys. (The fact that Kelly couldn't care less about privacy is irrelevant, since androids claim total equality with flesh-and-blood human beings, including the right to share our neuroses. Kelly has full human-female status, and to treat her otherwise would be to commit racial discrimination. Right?)

What Dr. Schein proposed to do was put all the human males—himself, Leroy Chang, Saul Shahmoon, and myself—into one bubble, and Jan and Kelly into the other. Okay, that got around the elemental decency situation. *But—*

Jan and Kelly would thereby have to bunk with the aliens, several of whom were males of their species. (Steen Steen and 408b could be excluded from that category, Steen because he/she is of both sexes and

408b because it doesn't seem to be of either.) I guess some stuffy souls on Earth might get upset that Jan and Kelly would be dressing and undressing in front of males of any sort, even alien males. (They might get upset about Jan, anyway; stuffy types don't seem to worry much about the living conditions of androids.) However, that wasn't what troubled Dr. Schein. He knew that Kelly is without inhibitions; and that Jan, while she's been observing the usual taboos around the four human males, doesn't really think that Pilazinool or Dr. Horkkk or Mirrik pose any threat to her virtue. He was worried about offending the aliens, though. If Jan observed clothing taboos with us and not with them, couldn't that be construed as meaning that she regarded them as second-class life-forms? Shouldn't a girl be modest in front of *all* intelligent creatures, or else none? Where is the equality of galactic races, of which we hear so much, in such a case?

I can hear you snorting with amused impatience and giving one of your typical common-sense answers. You might have pointed out that none of the aliens wear clothes themselves, or have any kind of privacy taboos, or even remotely understand why it is that Earthfolk feel they must cover certain parts of their bodies. You might also have noted that galactic equality doesn't have anything to do with sex—which is at the bottom of our thing about clothes—and that it is perfectly proper for a girl to be modest with males of her own species without at the same time seeming to put down males of some other species. But common sense, Lorie, doesn't always rule the universe. Dr. Schein had a long huddle with Jan, and then conferred with Saul Shahmoon and Leroy Chang, and finally—very nervously —took the matter to Dr. Horkkk. Who thought it was so wildly funny that he tied all his arms into knots, which is how the people of Thhh register uncontrollable laughter. He expressed the belief that none of the non-humans would take offense if the girls failed to be properly demure with them.

And so it was settled. What a bunch of chimpos we Earthers can be about these primitive idiocies!

The four of us got Mirrik the bulldozer for a bunkmate, since there wasn't room for him with the others. Jan and Kelly bunked with Dr. Horkkk, Pilazinool, 408b, and Steen Steen. For all I know they had wild orgies over there all night.

I slept poorly. It wasn't just Mirrik's fragrance, which I'll adapt to in time, but the excitement that got to me. Sleeping a hundred meters away from a treasure trove a billion years old, piled high with the artifacts left behind by the mightiest and most advanced race the universe has ever known. What wonders will we find in that hillside?

I'll know soon. It's morning, now. Pale, straggly light is coming over the horizon. I was the first one up in our dorm; but when I came outside I found Dr. Horkkk doing some kind of weird calisthenics, and Pilazinool sitting on the ground stripped down to a torso and one arm, polishing his other limbs, while 408b was meditating. Those aliens don't sleep much.

An hour from now we'll tackle the site. More news later.

three

We've been at it a week. No luck. I almost think we've been hoaxed.

The site is a hillside outcropping exposed by recent erosion, as I think I may have said already. The top forty meters of countryside here did not exist when the High Ones had their camp on Higby V; all of this gritty, sandy yellowish soil piled up hundreds of millions of years after their time, deposited by wind and flood in the long-ago days when this planet still had weather. Then after we got here and reintroduced weather, the topsoil started to erode, permitting the discovery last year of characteristic High Ones artifacts. Fine.

Then Dr. Schein and a couple of grad students from Marsport came here last year to do the preliminary survey. They went into action with neutrino magnetometers and sonar probes and density rods, and calculated that the zone of High Ones occupation constituted a large lenticular cone running deep into the hillside. Fine. They covered the whole site with a plastic weather shield and went away to raise funds for a full-scale excavation operation, in which I have been allowed to take part. Fine. We are here. Fine. We have begun the customary resurvey procedures. Fine. Fine. Fine. We haven't found a thing. Not so fine.

I don't understand what's wrong.

What we have to do, basically, is very gently lift off the top of the hillside so we'll have access to what was the surface of the ground a billion years ago. Then we gently work our way down, layer by layer, to the High Ones strata. Then we gently take everything out, one scrap at a time, recording relative positions in a dozen different ways. If we're gentle enough we may learn something about the High Ones here. If we aren't gentle, our names will go down in the black book of archaeology alongside the spineless sposhers who took that Martian temple apart to see what was underneath it, and couldn't get it back together again. Or the zoobies who found the key to Plorvian hieroglyphics and dropped it overboard in a methane ocean. Or the feeby quonker who stepped on the Dsmaalian Urn. The first rule in archaeology is: Be careful with the evidence. It isn't replaceable.

No, that's the second rule. The first one is: Find your evidence.

We commenced by scanning the top of the hill. We found some intrusive Higby V burials up there, maybe 150,000 years old, dating from the last epoch before this planet lost its atmosphere. The natives of this planet were of no special cultural interest, never having got much past the level of Stone Age man, and as Dr. Schein had already made clear, we are here exclusively to study High Ones remains. Still, once we stumbled onto this Higby V stuff, we had to treat it with some respect, since it might be somebody else's specialty. So Mirrik reverently cleared the site, Kelly Watchman got to work vacuum-coring, and we transferred the whole business to an open space back of the hill, where Steen Steen and I sealed it up and marked it for future reference.

There weren't any other irrelevant deposits in the upper part of the hill. Luckily. The next stage was to lift most of the remaining overburden. ("Overburden" is one of those zooby archaeological terms of which you're always cranking, Lorie. It means the burden of soil or gravel or rock or whatever that's on top of what you want to excavate. I know it sounds dumb, but what the zog, it's part of the professional jargon.)

To clear overburden quickest, you use a hydraulic lift. This is nothing more than a highly directional sort of hose-and-pump deal, which you snake into your hillside at just the right angle. Turn the water on and zit! The overburden is sliced off and sloshed away. Dr. Schein and Leroy Chang spent half a day computing velocities and lift angles; then we ran the pipes into the hill, hitched up the compressors, and in five minutes succeeded in cutting off the top twenty meters or so of the hill. In theory we now had a clear shot at our site.

In theory.

In practice, not the case. Our modern gadgets deceive us into thinking archaeology is easy, sometimes. But gadgets may err, and in many ways we are not too far removed from the innocent pioneers of four hundred years ago, who bashed around with picks and shovels until they found what they were after.

Our trouble seems to be that Dr. Schein's survey of last year was off by a bit, and that the degree of error is variable, which is to say he was wronger in some places than in others. This is forgivable: an underground survey is a tricky thing even when you have neutrino magnetometers and sonar probes and density rods. Still, it's a pain. We know that a terrific cache of High Ones things is right in front of us. (At least, we *think* we know it.) But we haven't found it yet.

Mirrik labors heroically to clear the remaining overburden. This has to be done manually, because we're too close to the supposed upper strata of High Ones occupation to dare use anything as violent as the hydraulic lift. Kelly hovers just back of Mirrik's huge left shoulder, taking core samplings now and then. The rest of us haul dirt, fidget, speculate, play chess, and crank a good deal.

The weather doesn't help. At least our work is conducted under the weather shield, but that protects only the site and those actually examining it. In order to get from shack to site we have to cross a hundred meters of open ground, with one chance out of four that it will be raining, three chances out of four that a strong wind will be blowing, and five chances out of four that the air will be bone-chillingly cold. When it rains, it doesn't drizzle. The wind unfailingly carries tons of sand and grit. And the cold is the sort of cold that doesn't just bother you, it persecutes you. Some of us don't mind it, like Pilazinool, although he's having tremendous trouble with sand in his joints. Dr. Horkkk comes from a cold planet—you can even have cold planets around a blazing star like Rigel, if you're far enough out—and he rather enjoys a brisk breeze. Mirrik doesn't mind because his hide is so thick. The rest of us are a little unhappy.

The landscape is no source of cheer. Some trees and shrubs, chosen for their ability to hold down topsoil, not for their beauty. Low hills. Craters. Puddles.

Dad would be sniggering up his sleeve if he knew the dark thoughts I've thought all week. "Serve the slicy idiot right!" he'd say. "Let him marinate in his archaeology! Let him ossify in it!"

You were lucky, Lorie. You missed the really nasty family conferences dealing with my choice of a profession. Dad hates to stir a fuss when we're visiting you. Even so, you got a good dose of the quarreling, but it wasn't a snip of what went on at home.

I have to say I was awfully disappointed in Dad when he started all that cranking about my being an archaeologist.

"Get a real job!" he kept yelling. "Be an ultradrive pilot, if you want to see the galaxy! You know what kind of stash they make? The pension rights? They get sore thumbs from all the spending they do. Or interplanetary law, now, *there's* a profession! Alien torts and malfeasances! Hypothecation of assets on non-verbal worlds! Infinite possibilities, Tom, infinite! Why, I knew a lawyer on Capella XII, he did nothing but color-change suits and metamorphoses, and he had a ten-year backlog with six clerks!"

If you ever play this back, Lorie, I hope you appreciate the skill with which I imitate Our Lord And Master's voice. I get just the right tone of hearty manliness mixed with stuffy hypocrisy, don't I? No, blot that. Dad's not really a hypocrite. He's consistent to his own rules.

We all knew he wasn't the intellectual type, though I at least always felt that despite his extreme concern with piling up stash and keeping a busy thumb, he had some interest in the finer values. He did get a degree from Fentnor, after all, and even though it was in Business Administration they don't let you escape from Fentnor illiterate. I also felt that Dad was far from being the kind of reactionary vidj that tries to dictate his son's professional choice. He always struck me as a live and let live type.

So it hurt when he came down so hard against my going into archaeology.

No secret what he really wants, which is for me to follow him into the real-estate business and eventually to take over from him. But real estate sings no songs to me, and I made that clear to him, didn't I, by the time I was sixteen? Dad gets his zingers, not to mention much stash, from building his instant slums out of parapithlite sheeting on faraway worlds, and I suppose for him this is a creative thing. I admit some of his projects have been ingenious, such as the chain of floating houses on that gas-giant world in the Capella system, or the high-grav shopping center with interlocking centrifuges that he whipped up for the Muliwomps. Nevertheless I have always lacked a craving for this entire pocket.

Anyway, why should I go into a "useful" or "profitable" line of work, to quote two of Dad's favorite adjectives? What better justification for his bulging bank accounts than that they allowed his son to dedicate himself to the pursuit of pure knowledge?

Such as the digging up of old odds and ends on miserable cold stormy planets.

Enough. I need not yammer to you about Dad's obtuseness, since I think you share my feelings and—as usual—are 100 percent on my side. Dad went his way, I went mine, and perhaps he'll soften up and forgive me after a while for turning my back on color-change litigation and housing projects, and if not, I will somehow avoid starvation anyway, doing what I most enjoy doing, which is archaeologizing.

Though I will not pretend that I've enjoyed this current job so far.

I will take a positive attitude. I will tell myself that we'll hit the right level any day.

.   .   .

Three-hour intermission there, during which I helped to perform some hard, dull, valuable work.

What we did was get fiber telescopes into the hillside to see what's in there. These are long strands of glass which transmit an optically undistorted image from end to end, given the right illumination. Getting them into the hillside involved drilling holes, which Kelly took care of with her vacuum equipment; this had to be done with unusual care, since the drill might blunder right into the site we're looking for and chop it up some.

I may have underestimated Kelly. She handles those corers beautifully.

Kelly perforated the hill for us; then we mounted the fiber telescopes on sprocket wheels and fed them ticklishly into the ground. We put four in altogether, spaced twenty meters apart; Jan and I worked together on one wheel.

Now the telescopes are in place. The big shots are peering into the heart of the mound. Night is falling, and it's raining again. I'm in the dorm, dictating this. If my voice is a little low, it's because I don't want to disturb Saul and Mirrik, who are playing chess. It's astonishing to watch somebody as huge as Mirrik moving chess pieces around with the tip of a tusk.

Jan is running toward our shack from the dig site. She looks excited. She's calling something to us, but I can't hear her through the bubble wall.

      .   .   .

One hour later. Night, now. What Jan was trying to say was that they hit paydirt. The telescopes show the location of the High Ones cache. We weren't more than a dozen meters off course. For some reason we had misinterpreted the survey figures and were coming in on a tilt, but we can correct for that now.

It's too late to do any digging tonight. First thing in the morning we'll plot a whole new survey graph so that we have the position down perfectly. Then we'll finally be ready to start real work, with all of the preliminaries out of the way.

The whole team is over in our dorm right now. Outside it's pouring again. Everyone's tense and jumpy. Dr. Horkkk keeps pacing around in that weird precise way of his—a dozen steps, turn, a dozen steps back, turn, mathematically calculated so that he covers the same distance down to the millimeter. Steen Steen and Leroy Chang are following along behind him, having some kind of argument about High Ones linguistics. Pilazinool and Kelly Watchman are playing chess, which as you've guessed is our big recreation here. Kelly got very wet coming back from the site and has stripped down to her pretty pink synthetic skin, which has Leroy Chang disturbed; he keeps peering over his shoulder at her. So much for all that elaborate stuff about modesty. Kelly *is* a handsome wench, of course, but it quonks me how Leroy can get so excited about something that came out of a vat of chemicals. Maybe she's naked, but she isn't real, and that takes some of the thrill out of the nakedness. Pilazinool has done *his* kind of strip routine too: he's down to head and torso, and one arm to make the moves, while the rest of his body is lying in a mixed-up heap next to his bench. Now and then he screws one of his legs back on, or takes off an antenna, or otherwise fissions around with himself in his nervous way. He's losing the chess game, incidentally.

Dr. Schein is running scanner tapes of previous High Ones excavations, and is discussing tomorrow's digging techniques with Mirrik, who has plenty to say. Saul Shahmoon has one of his stamp albums out and is showing his prize specimens to 408b and Jan, who don't look very interested. And I'm sitting off in one corner talking into a message cube.

The evening seems endless.

Is it ever like this for you, Lorie? Even after all these years I don't really know how you work inside. I mean, lying there, hardly able to move, getting your food through tubes, no way even to go to the window and see what the weather's like. Yet I've never seen you bored or impatient or even depressed. If you were some kind of mental vegetable, I could understand it. But your mind is active and alert and probably in most ways a better mind than mine. Here I am—here we all are—counting minutes until morning and sick of waiting. And there you are, with nothing to look forward to except another day of the same, keeping cheerful.

Is it the TP that does it? I guess it is. Being able to rove all through the universe in your mind. Talking with friends on a thousand different planets, seeing strange scenes through their eyes, finding out everything about everything without leaving your bed at all. You can't ever be bored or lonely for long. You just have to tune in on some other TP and you've got company and entertainment.

I've always felt sorry for you, Lorie. Me being so healthy and active, going everywhere, doing so much, and you tied down to your hospital room, and yet we're twins, who are supposed to share so much. That's the ironic part. But tonight I wonder whether I ought to pity you or envy you. I can walk; you can soar from star to star via your TP powers, no limits. Which of us is the real cripple?

Idle thoughts on a long night, nothing else.

.   .   .

Jan is tired of looking at Saul's stamps. I heard her ask him to go for a walk with her, but he said no, he's got some cataloging to do. So Jan came over and asked me instead. Second choice, as usual.

We'll go out and stroll a while, unless it's still raining. She's a nice kid. This fixation she has on Saul makes no sense to me—he's twice her age, obviously a confirmed bachelor, and must have been frightened by a woman at an early age, judging by the way he hides behind those stamp albums—but maybe Jan's got a need for pursuing shy older men. We're each of us chimpo in our special way, I guess. Anyhow, if she wants to walk a while, why should I say no? It's a way of passing time.

So I'll wrap up this cube here. Perhaps next time I'll tell you how we uncovered the tomb of the Emperor of the High Ones and found him still alive, in suspended animation. Or how we found the Secret Treasure of the High Ones, fifty billion credits worth of uranium. Fantasy comes cheap on a dull night. Tomorrow arrives the moment of truth at last. Out into the cold and dark, now. Off.

four

So we started digging, and right away we came to this sleek solid plutonium sarcophagus with a platinum button on its side, and Dr. Horkkk pushed the button and the coffin popped open, and inside it we saw the Emperor of the High Ones, who came out of suspended animation and sat up and said, "Greetings, O beings of a distant future age!"

So we began to follow this narrow winding tunnel through the hill, and Kelly cored into a side passage where there was this vault of blue fusion-glass, and upon command of "Open, Sesame," the vault door swung back and we saw, neatly stacked, the cubes of uranium that we realized had to be the imperial treasure of the High Ones, worth at least fifty billion credits.

So we—

Well, as a matter of fact nothing like that has happened yet. Or is really likely to happen. But I thought I'd start this letter off with some zing. It is true, though, that we've been excavating for several days and that the site looks promising. More than promising—downright exciting.

This is the twenty-third High Ones site that's been discovered. Possibly you know that the first site came to light a dozen years ago in the Syrtis Major region of Mars and was mistaken at first for the remains of some extremely ancient Martian culture. But nothing else like it turned up on Mars, whereas a couple dozen sites very similar to it have been found on widely spaced planets occupying a sphere with a radius of about a hundred light-years. So we know that the people who left these deposits must have been members of some galactic race that covered a lot of territory in its travels. Very early in the story, the newstape reporters christened them the High Ones, and the name has stuck. Even we archaeologists use it. It isn't very scientific, but somehow it seems appropriate.

All the High Ones sites found so far follow the same general pattern. That is, they represent outposts rather than permanent settlements, as if the High Ones had sent roving bands of explorers all over the galaxy and these explorers had stopped off at a given planet for twenty or thirty or fifty years, then moved along. At each site archaeologists have uncovered typical High Ones artifacts—intricate, incomprehensible objects, usually well preserved, downright baffling in their function. The workmanship is superb. They used gold and metallic plastics as their materials, usually, and some of the artifacts seem almost new.

They aren't new. They come to us across a billion years.

We have fairly exact methods for dating ancient sites, and we know that the High Ones lived on Mars approximately a billion years back, with a possible range of error of ten million years, or one percent. The other sites have been dated at various points from 1,100,000,000 years ago to 850,000,000 years ago. Which tells us two significant things:

—That the High Ones had developed a galactic civilization at a time when nothing more complex than crabs and snails had evolved on Earth.

—That the High Ones' culture underwent no significant changes over a span of *a quarter of a billion years*—which indicates a rigid, conservative, fully mature civilization that endured for a period of time that makes me dizzy to think about. We look upon the ancient Egyptians as a stable bunch because their civilization remained basically the same for about three thousand years. Zit! What's three thousand years against 250,000,000?

The High Ones have handed us a huge batch of puzzles. Such as the question of their origin. We haven't yet found any High Ones outposts beyond that hundred-light-year radius. Of course, we haven't done much real exploring beyond that radius ourselves, although we've had ships out as far as eight hundred light-years from Earth. But the total absence of High Ones traces on all the outer worlds examined so far is odd.

One school of thought argues that the High Ones are native to our galaxy and originated on one of the planets inside the hundred-light-year zone. The fact that we haven't yet found anything like a major city of the High Ones is irrelevant; sooner or later we'll come upon the planet from which all the scouting parties set out. Dr. Horkkk is the leading exponent of this theory. In our group Leroy Chang supports him.

The other notion is that the High Ones came from someplace far out—100,000 light-years away, maybe, at the other end of our galaxy—and hopped over most of the intervening stars to make a long and leisurely exploration of our little corner of the universe. Maybe they even were extra-galactic, say, from the Magellanic Clouds, 200,000 light-years away, and devoted a couple hundred million years to an examination of our galaxy. Dr. Schein buys the extra-galactic theory. So does Saul Shahmoon.

Naturally, Dr. Schein and Dr. Horkkk don't ever cross swords openly over their differences of opinion. It just isn't done. When two top scientists disagree, they do so in the pages of learned journals, with festoons of footnotes and a lot of carefully antiseptic prose that says, in not so many words, "My respected opponent in this discussion is a chimpo quonker." If they happen to meet face to face, or especially if they find themselves on the same field expedition, they remain icily polite, never even mentioning the issue in dispute, although under their skulls they can't help thinking, "My admired colleague here is a chimpo quonker."

The rest of us aren't bound by the code duello that governs men at the summit of a field. So we've taken sides and we yammer a lot about our ideas—more for the sport of it than anything else, since we have no real knowledge to go by.

"Obviously extra-galactic," says 408b crisply. "The total absence of evidence except in one insignificant corner of the galaxy means that they must have come from—"

"Cut it," Mirrik bellows. "One of these days we'll find their home world, right close at hand, and—"

"Nonsense!"

"Feeby foolery!"

"Unscientific blenking!"

"A lot of silly fission!"

"Ignorance!"

"Idiotic slice!"

"Intellectual nilliness!"

And so the quonking goes, far into the night. Mirrik and Steen Steen back Dr. Horkkk on the local-origin theory, and so does Jan Mortenson, although not very firmly. 408b and I line up with Dr. Schein and the extra-galactic-origin theory. Kelly Watchman is neutral, because it's not in the nature of androids to get excited about theories when they lack enough facts to make a logical judgment. Pilazinool, our specialist in intuitive analysis, is also silent on the subject. I'm sure he has his private opinions, but it isn't his habit to air them until he feels ready to issue a complete statement. When he *does* issue a complete statement, it isn't intended as a topic for debate; it's meant as The Word. Pilazinool therefore is careful not to try to give The Word until he knows what it is.

Why am I on Dr. Schein's side, you ask? How can I

be on anybody's side when we don't really know a thing?

Simple. You know I have a romantic streak, Lorie. Otherwise I wouldn't be out here doing what I'm doing, in defiance of my father's notions of what I should be making out of my life. And so I automatically incline toward the theory that lights the most lights in my imagination.

If the High Ones did originate someplace within a hundred light-years of Earth, they have to be extinct now. If they still existed we'd certainly have bumped into them by this time.

If they came from some other galaxy, though, they may still be thriving out there somewhere. I like to think that they are. A race that can last a few hundred million years without blowing itself up—and we know that they lasted at least that long—can probably be considered just about immortal, as races go. And so, if Dr. Schein's ideas are correct, it's at least possible that the High Ones inhabit some other galaxy, living in all their ancient splendor, and that we may some day stumble upon them, who knows where? The Magellanic Clouds, M31 in Andromeda, the spiral galaxy M104 in Virgo, anywhere.

Let me quickly add that neither Dr. Schein nor any other reputable archaeologist has suggested that the High Ones still survive. A billion years is a long time even for a civilization of superbeings to endure. It is strictly my own wild notion that they linger on. The night I took my walk with Jan, I let a little of this emerge, and she was appalled.

"Nothing lasts a billion years, Tom!"

"You're judging by Earth standards. Just because we're newcomers to the universe, that doesn't mean—"

"But there isn't any intelligent race anywhere that's remotely that old!" she protested. "The Shilamakka are about the oldest race in the galaxy, aren't they? And they evolved only about fifty million years ago. Whereas our own species doesn't even go back half a million years. And the Calamorians are even newer, and—"

"We have proof that the High Ones were able to survive across a span of 250 million years, Jan. So we know they had staying power. They could very well still—"

"What about evolutionary changes? In a billion years they'd have evolved out of all recognition!"

"Don't you think they could control their own genetic flow?" I asked. "A conservative race like that wouldn't allow random mutations. They'd keep themselves intact and unchanging."

"And what about the natural resources of their home planet? Wouldn't those have been exhausted long ago?"

"Who says they're still living on their original planet?"

Jan wasn't convinced. I have to confess that I wasn't, either. The thought that one species can keep a civilization running for as much as a million years is more than an Earthborn type like me can comprehend. To talk about survival over a *billion* years—it sploshes the mind just to imagine it.

And yet—Lorie, I *want* them still to be out there somewhere. I can't bear to believe that such greatness could ever have come to an end and vanished from the universe. The last of the High Ones, the death of a civilization millions of years old, no momentum left, cultural exhaustion, maybe—I reject it. Perhaps because to accept the passing of the High Ones means to accept the passing of Earthman culture some day. None of us ever believes in the possibility of his own death. Certainly not in the death of his species, his civilization. And if I believe in the immortality of the human race, as I can't help doing, how can I believe that this much greater race of High Ones could have been mortal? No. I tell myself that they cling to existence far from here, in another galaxy, even though they may have forgotten how at one time they visited a neighboring galaxy where intelligent life hadn't yet evolved. Ours.

There. That's your chimpo brother talking, handing out the same sort of zooby romanticism that he always peddled. You used to tell me that I didn't have the true scientific attitude of objectivity. Maybe you were right.

.   .   .

I see that I haven't managed to say much about what we've accomplished here so far.

The basic thing about working at High Ones sites is that they're so fantastically old that the usual techniques of archaeology can't be applied. We're paleo-archaeologists rather than archaeologists. We can't just clear sand or dirt out of a site, the way the boys do on a dig in Egypt or New Mexico, and start hauling up artifacts. Over a billion years sand or dirt turn to *stone*.

We have to carve all our finds out of solid rock.

For this we can use standard methods, up to a point. We clear away overburdens of soil with power shovels, with hand tools, and with bulldozers, including Dinamonians like Mirrik. When the heart of the site is exposed, though, we have to use vacuum-corers. These peel the rock away literally a molecule at a time, laying bare the artifacts we're after. If your vacuum-corer operator is a little on the spineless side, he's likely to chew up a few molecules of the artifact too, before he can stop.

So far Kelly has been just about perfect. She did cut into one very minor deposit, but that's forgivable; otherwise she's stripped the site with real skill. I take back all the stuff I was saying in the first cube about the inadequacies of an android vacuum-corer operator.

It took the better part of a week to get rid of the overburden, and another few days passed before we began to hit artifacts. This site is the biggest High Ones camp ever discovered, running for more than a hundred meters into the hillside. At this point we have collected a lot of standard stuff, debris discarded around the periphery of the camp, such things as—

·*Inscription nodes.* These are plastic tubes, about the size and shape of a cigar, usually deep green in color but sometimes blue. Along one side they bear an inscription in High Ones hieroglyphics, customarily consisting of seventy-five to a hundred symbols. At unpredictable intervals the inscriptions fade and new ones appear. This may happen when we hand a tube to someone else, when we tilt it, when the person holding it undergoes a sudden change of mood, or when it starts or stops raining. On the other hand, sometimes it is impossible to induce any change in the inscription even when all of these things occur simultaneously. Hundreds of inscription nodes have been uncovered at each High Ones site. Some have been opened; they have no moving parts and appear to be solid plastic all the way through. We understand what makes the inscriptions come and go about as thoroughly as a Neanderthal would understand where a television image comes from. We also are unable to decipher the inscriptions.

· *Commemorative plaques*. These are medals of some sort, about the size of large coins and stamped from some rustproof white metal. Heaps of them litter all High Ones sites. On one side they bear the image of what we assume is a High One: a humanoid creature with four arms, two legs, and a dome-shaped head. On the reverse side is an inscription in the same symbols found on the nodes. The melting point of the metal used in these plaques is upward of 3500 degrees; the metal is so extraordinarily hard that we don't see how it could have been stamped. Chemical analysis has not revealed the nature of the alloy used.

· *Puzzle-boxes*. Just as the name implies: these are interlocking sheets of metal arranged in a variosity of disturbing patterns. The simplest ones are moebius strips, which are just flat lengths of metal with a twist in the middle and the ends joined, so that you can run your finger along one side, keep going past the twist, and end up on the other side without ever having lifted your finger. That is, the moebius strip is truly two-dimensional, since it only has one side. Okay?

Then there are klein bottles, which are three-dimensional containers that loop back on themselves so that they also have just one surface. Also there are tesseracts, which are structures with four spatial dimensions —a tesseract is to a cube as a cube is to a square, yes? If you look at a tesseract the right way, you'll understand, but I don't recommend trying. And then there are puzzle-boxes that don't fit any mathematical theory, that fit together in odd ways so that you can trace a path down one side, and up another, and then you come to a place where the surface disappears and you're somewhere else. About a dozen different kinds of puzzle-boxes are known. Maybe the High Ones used them for intellectual amusement. There are plenty of them here, in surprisingly good shape.

· *Miscellaneous artifacts.* These include dials, levers, buttons that glow in the dark, small items of what we think is jewelry, prisms, gears, tubes that heat up at one end when a finger is placed at the other, and a lot more. Everything is glossy and beautifully made, even the miniatures; and everything has stood up well to a billion years of geological pressure.

As we proceed inward toward the center of the deposit, we are collecting an amazing quantity of this stuff. The density of discarded material is higher here than anywhere else, leading us to hope that this was some special place and that we're likely to find something of special significance inside. Such as a tomb. We have never, you know, discovered the physical remains of a High One. Even a fossil skeleton can't be expected to last a billion years—not intact, anyway—but it was within the grasp of High Ones technology to build a metal or plastic container capable of standing up to any kind of conditions, judging by the survival characteristics of these artifacts. Yet nowhere at any of the twenty-three sites have we come upon a burial, or even a trace of one. Since each of these sites was occupied for several decades, it's not unreasonable to think that some members of the expedition must have died in the course of duty.

Were dead High Ones taken to the home planet for burial?

Were the bodies of the dead cremated right down to the atomic level?

Or . . . did the High Ones have such enormous individual life-spans that it just wasn't statistically probable for any of them to die in any fifty-year occupation of a given site?

We don't know. But we'd love to find out for sure what the High Ones looked like.

Progress here is necessarily slow. We all dig, even the big bosses, but we can't cover more than a few cubic meters a day. Mirrik goes first, bulldozing away the overburden. Kelly moves in with her vacuum-corers and slices off a little rock. The rest of us pitch in to free whatever artifacts she's turned up. Before we can lift anything, we have to photograph it and record its position. Then it goes over to the laboratory, where Saul Shahmoon makes chronological studies. He hasn't finished dating this site yet, but he's already hinted that it's a pretty late one, maybe no more than 900,000,000 years old. Next, everything bearing an inscription goes to Dr. Horkkk, who collects the data and feeds it into his computer. 408b, whose specialty is paleotechnology, checks everything out mechanically, looking for insight into the ways things work. Pilazinool, meanwhile, snoops around here and there, trying to pick up the scattered clues that will allow him to make one of his intuitive judgments.

We all have this strange and mysterious feeling that we're on the brink of something important. Nobody knows why. Maybe it's just overoptimism.

We work hard. Archaeology is mostly a sore back and aching fingers. The romance gets into it afterward, when the newstape boys write their stories. In the evenings we rest, play a lot of chess, argue some, listen to the rain. I find that hour by hour I'm often bored, but that the overall effect of being here is terrifically exciting.

.   .   .

We are having a problem with Mirrik. If it isn't solved soon he may be dismissed from the expedition. Which would be sad, because in his ponderous way he's a delightful vidj.

I told you that Mirrik is in the alcoholism pocket, so to speak. He goes not for booze but for flowers; something in the nectar of an ordinary blossom clangs him with terrific impact. The metabolic effect of a flower on a Dinamonian must be tremendous, far more potent than alcohol is with us, since a couple of mouthfuls of flowers are sufficient to give all of Mirrik's tonnage a colossal charge.

Bleak as this place is, it's got some flowers. One of the terraforming engineers must have had a poetic soul —he planted a grove of frostflowers about two kilometers from where we're digging. The plants took hold in a few sheltered places. Mirrik, who needs plenty of exercise and likes to go on long rambling solitary roamings, found them.

I was the first to discover his secret.

One afternoon last week I was going off duty after finishing my stint at the dig when I saw Mirrik come capering toward me. He'd had a couple of hours of free time too. As he approached the site, he leaped up and tried to click his front feet together. That didn't work, and he landed in a tangle. He got up, ran in a circle, tried it again. Again he failed. He saw me and giggled. Imagine ten tons of giggling Dinamonian! He clicked his tusks playfully. He wobbled toward me, grabbed me amiably with his arms, and made me spin. This so amused him that he began a rhythmic pounding of his feet. The ground shook.

"Hello, Tommo, howzaboy?" He winked. He breathed in my face. "Good old Tommo. Letz danz, Tommo!"

"Mirrik, you're tanked!" I told him.

"Nonzenz." He prodded me playfully in the ribs with his tusks. "Danz! Danz!"

I jumped back. "Where did you find flowers?"

"No flowerz here. Juzzt happpppy!"

His muzzle was golden with frostflower pollen. I frowned and brushed it off. Mirrik giggled again. I said, "Hold still, you oversized sposher! If Dr. Horkkk sees you like this, he'll flay you!"

Mirrik wanted to stop off in the laboratory to argue philosophy with Pilazinool. I discouraged him from that. Then it began to rain, which sobered him a little, enough to see that he might get in trouble if one of the bosses found him. "Walk with me until I zober up," he said, and I did, and we discussed the evolution of religious mysticism until his head was clear. As we returned to the camp he said sadly, "I grieve for my weakness, Tom. But I feel I have learned restraint with your help. I won't visit the frostflower patch again."

He came in drunk the next day too.

I was in the lab, cleaning and sorting the latest haul of broken inscription nodes and battered plaques, when a voice from outside roared as though over a cosmic loudspeaker:

> Come, fill the Cup, and in the fire of Zpring
> Your Winter-garment of Repentanz fling;
> The Bird of Time has but a little way
> To flutter—and the Bird is on the Wing.

"It's the Rubaiyat!" cried Jan, entranced.

"It's Mirrik!" I gasped.

Dr. Horkkk looked up grimly from his computer input. Dr. Schein frowned. 408b muttered something in disgust; it has no use for such foibles as this.

Mirrik went on:

> Zome for the Gloriez of Thiz Worrrld; and zome
> Zigh for the Prophet's Paradizzzze to come;
> Ah, take the Cash, and let the Crrredit go,
> Nor heed the rumble of a diztant Drrrum!

Jan and I hustled out of the lab and found Mirrik tusking up the turf in front of the building. Crushed frostflower blossoms were sticking out behind his ears, and his whole face was dusted with pollen. He looked mournfully at me for an instant, as though a sober Mirrik were trying to peer out behind the drunken mask; then he giggled again and continued:

Ah, my Belovéd, fill the Cup that clears
Today of pazzt Regrets and future Fears:
    Tomorrrrow!—Why, Tomorrow I may be
Myzelf with Yezterday's Zev'n thousand Years.

"Tomorrow you may be on your way home," I said sharply. "For Omar's sake, Mirrik, get out of here! If Dr. Horkkk sees you—"

Too late.

That night Mirrik had a long conference with our bosses, who are afraid that he'll show up really glapped some day and wreck the camp. A drunken Dinamonian is about as safe to have around as a runaway rocket, and unless Mirrik can lay off the frostflowers he'll be shipped out. 408b had a sweeter suggestion: simply chain Mirrik up, like an unruly bull, when he isn't working. Kindly old 408b always goes straight to the humane solution.

Most of us try to cover for Mirrik when he comes into camp loaded. We walk him sober, or steer him away from the bubbleshacks if he tries to enter, or otherwise protect him against himself. But we aren't fooling anyone. Dr. Schein and Dr. Horkkk are both worried about this business. And when those two agree on anything, it means trouble.

        ·   ·   ·

Leroy Chang thinks I'm having a love affair with Jan, by the way. That's pretty funny.

I did take a long walk with her one night, I admit.

And several shorter walks. Can I help it if I like her company? She's the only female human being here —whoops, I mean, not counting Kelly Watchman! Anyway, she's the only person here of my own age except Steen Steen, for whom I don't care very much, and she's the only girl here, Kelly being past ninety and android besides, and I have more in common with her than I do with, say, 408b or Dr. Horkkk. So I naturally tend to spend time with Jan.

But a love affair?

Leroy is jealous of phantoms. He's one of these twitchy bachelor types who chases girls compulsively, usually without much luck, and his score with Jan is zero. She regards him—pretty accurately—as a creep. Since he can't accept that as his explanation for his lack of success with her, he has made up a better one, which is that since I am younger and taller and dumber than he is, Jan in her postadolescent shallowness has fallen for me.

His way of expressing his resentment is to poke me in the ribs and leer and say, "You two had a hot time last night, huh? I bet you did! You're a real biology artist, eh, kid?"

"Get sploshed, Leroy," I tell him amiably. "Jan and I aren't in the same orbit."

"You say it with a straight face, too. But you don't fool me. When you bring her back, she's got that steamy, excited look on her face—a man of the worlds like me, I know right away what you've been up to."

"Usually we've been discussing the day's finds."

"But of course! Of *course*!" He lowers his voice. "Listen, Tommo, I can't blame you for doing all the passionating you can, but have a heart! There are other men on this expedition, and females are in short supply." A coarse wink. "Mind if *I* take her behind the rockpile one of these nights?"

That's me, Tom Rice, villainous monopolizer of women! Would you believe it? There isn't any tactful way that I can explain to Leroy that he's his own worst enemy, so far as his relationship with Jan goes: that if he weren't so pushy and possessive and grabby and raw, she might be able to tolerate him a little. Certainly it isn't that I've locked up her affections, because, no matter what Leroy thinks, my dealings with Jan have been those of brother to sister.

Well . . . more or less. . . .

She is still totally tickled toward Saul Shahmoon, and I blush to confess that most of the time when I'm alone with Jan she talks about how wonderful Saul is and how terrible it is that he won't fall for her. She praises his clarity of mind, his neatness, his suave Mediterranean good looks, his cool self-possessed manner, and his other virtues. She laments that his strange obsession with philately leaves him too busy for love, and asks my advice on how best to win him over. Honest!

And Leroy Chang keeps insisting that Jan and I hold orgies back of the rockpile. . . .

Maybe I'll make a cough in her direction the next time we go strolling, you know? I mean, if Leroy has already tarnished our reputations with his insinuations and sniggerings, what's there to lose? She *is* an attractive girl. I have not taken any vows of chastity on this expedition. Besides, I'm getting awfully cranked about hearing her sing the splendors of Saul Shahmoon.

five

I personally discovered something of major importance this morning. And almost got myself fired for doing it. We still don't exactly understand what it is I found, but we know it's big. Possibly the biggest thing in High Ones archaeology up till now. Here's what happened—

After breakfast, five of us went out to the site to dig: me, Jan, Leroy Chang, Mirrik, and Kelly. At the present stage of things a five-man team is about as big as is efficient. The rest were in the lab, processing artifacts, dating things, running computer analyses, and doing other sorts of backstage work.

We are now pretty deep into the hillside, and the zone of High Ones occupation has widened considerably. Artifacts are thickly strewn about; we have more than a hundred inscription nodes already and a huge carton of plaques and puzzle boxes. All standard items, though; just more of them than usual.

It was a cool, rainy morning. They all are. We huddled under our weather shield and got to work. First Mirrik scooped out the backfill of soil that we had used to cover the actual excavation level. Then Kelly moved in with her vacuum-corer. The way we organized things, I got down in the hole to direct the work; Kelly crouched above me, drilling cores from the rock where I told her to; Mirrik stayed to my side, scooping up the debris with his tusks and carting it away; Jan ran the camera, filming everything in three dimensions; and Leroy, as the senior archaeologist of this particular team, kept a chart of all that went on.

For an hour the work was uneventful. Then we started coming around a zone of soft pinkish sandstone in which a batch of puzzle boxes were embedded. When you work hard enough and intensely enough, you start to become a kind of machine, sometimes, moving mechanically in an automatic rhythm, and that's how Kelly, Mirrik, and I were functioning. I'd point, Kelly would core, Mirrik would clear away; that exposed an artifact, which Jan photographed, Leroy charted, and I lifted carefully from its place to go into the collection box. Point, core, clear; photograph, chart, lift. Point, core, clear; photograph, chart, lift. Point, core, clear—

Something strange gleamed at me out of the sandstone.

It was a curved metal mass, gleaming brightly. From the gentleness of its curve I estimated that it was a globe of some kind at least one meter in diameter. It was fashioned of one of the customary gold alloys used by the High Ones for larger mechanisms; its surface was smooth in some places and covered with centimeter-high ridges in others.

"Bring that corer in here, Kelly!" I called. "Let's see what we've got!"

I guided her to the edges of the embedded artifact. Beautifully, delicately, she cored it free, exposing another few centimeters, and then a little more, and then still more. I scrabbled at the sand with my fingers, pushing it out of the way. Leroy didn't pay any attention to what we were doing; he was busy charting, or perhaps he was trying to get a little biology going with Jan. In any case both of them were well up above me on the rim of the pit and I was too involved in my digging to stop and see if Leroy had any special instructions for me.

"Here we go," I said to Kelly. "Follow the curve. See? Get the corer under here, and then—"

Kelly nodded. She looked tense and keyed-up with excitement, and when an android gets excited, it has to be something special. She gripped both handles of her corer and started drilling in from the side. The corer tip found a huge mass of sandstone and split it neatly. I started to heave debris, but Mirrik said, "That's too much for you, Tom. Get back." And jammed his tusks into the opening and pitched a half-ton of rubble out of sight.

Point, core, clear. Point, core, clear. I was drenched in sweat. Kelly, who doesn't sweat, somehow seemed flushed and sticky too. For ten minutes we went at it in a frenzied way, until half the globe was uncovered. I began to see a control panel and a variosity of knobs and buttons.

This is *not* the way to dig up something important. We were working in a mad rush, the three of us caught up in the thrill of a major find and unwilling or unable to slow up. I won't speak for Mirrik and Kelly, but I confess that I wanted to complete the excavation of this mysterious globe before any of the senior archaeologists could cut in on me. Unworthy motive! Also stupid chimposity and a display of colossal slice, since a mere apprentice like myself could easily have bungled the job and earned the curses of the whole profession.

I thought of all these things. But yet we went zooming ahead. Point, core, clear. Point, core, clear. Pointcoreclear. Pointcoreclear. Pointcoreclear.

I stopped for breath and looked up. Leroy and Jan weren't watching. They were biologizing. At least, Leroy in his subtle way had one hand on Jan's . . . well, hip . . . and the other groping for the magnet stud of her blouse, and he was trying to get his mouth on hers and she was fighting him off with clenched fists, and the whole thing had the look of a rape scene in the making. The chivalrous thing would have been for me to leap to the rim of the pit in one bound, cry, "Unhand her, knave!" and knock his teeth down his grinning glapper. But I told myself a) Jan can take care of herself, and b) while Leroy is wrestling with her he won't be able to meddle with what we're doing. So I was unchivalrous. Shame! Shame!

She fisted him in the gut. Leroy turned purple, doubled up, and dropped his chartbook into the pit.

Jan took off, streaking away into the rain. Leroy followed, yelling things like, "Jan! Jan! Just let me explain!"

"We're on our own," I said to Kelly and Mirrik. "Dig we onward!"

Dug we onward, unhindered. Kelly now was coring under the globe, and I tested it carefully, trying to rock it free of its embedment, but nothing going. Mirrik gave it a cautious nudge, too, and it tilted a little but remained in place. We could see that it was a beauty—so big I could barely span it with my arms, and covered along one side with all kinds of controls. Another five minutes, I figured, and we'd have it loose.

"Wait," Mirrik said. "At this moment I feel I should pray for the success of our labor."

Mirrik often does that. He's deeply religious, you know. He's a Paradoxian, worshiping the contrary forces of the universe, and bursts into prayer whenever those forces need to be placated, which is much of the time. Kelly drew back the corer and Mirrik delicately knelt in the pit, folding his huge legs under his massive body and letting the tips of his tusks rest on the globe. He began to groan and bellow in Dinamonian. Later I asked him to translate the prayer and he gave me this version:

O Father of confusions and sorrows, give us aid.
O Thou whose existence we doubt, doubt us not at such a time.
O ruler of the unrulable, O creator of the uncreated, O speaker of truths that lie, let our minds be clear and our aim accurate.

   O mystery in clarity, O foulness in purity, O darkness in light, comfort us and guide us and lead us.

Bring us not into error.

Cause us not to feel regret.

Remain with us now as on the first and last of all days.

Thou concealer of destinies and shatterer of patterns, be merciful, for in hatred lies love, in blindness lies sight, in falsehood lies righteousness. Amen. Amen. Amen."

You must agree with me that this is an odd kind of prayer. An odd kind of religion, too. The thing about aliens is that they tend to be so *alien.* But I have asked Mirrik to explain Paradoxianism to me one of these days, and perhaps he will.

When he finished his prayer he reared back, dug his tusks in under the big globe, uttered a moan of ecstasy, and pushed. The globe gave a little. He pushed again. The globe gave some more.

"Down here with the corer!" I yelled. "Just nip this little flange of stone away, and we've got it!"

In a kind of joyous insanity the three of us tugged, tusked, and cored at the bottom of the pit, jostling each other, jockeying for position, grabbing at the globe, altogether generating a chimpo scene of the first order. We thought the globe would come free, but it was more tightly embedded than we thought, and we came shudderingly close to damaging it in our lunatic urge to get it loose.

A cold, thin, furious voice said suddenly, "What are you *doing?* Idiots! Vandals! Criminals!"

I looked up. Dr. Horkkk peered down at me. His eyes were red with anger and seemed five times their normal size; he was waving all his arms at once and hopping around on three legs while wildly kicking himself with the fourth, which the people of Thhh do when they're upset; and both his talking mouth and his eating mouth were gaping in rage.

"We found this globe," I explained, "and now we're trying to clear the sandstone matrix, and—"

"You'll ruin it! Fools! Assassins!"

"Just another second now, Dr. Horkkk, and we'll have it."

You have to understand that while I held this discussion with Dr. Horkkk, Mirrik and Kelly and I were continuing to batter at the stone. If anything we grew more slapdash and hasty, as though the fate of the universe depended on lifting that globe from the stone within the next two minutes. Dr. Horkkk shrieked and screamed and capered. Dimly I heard him say, ". . . or I'll discharge the three of you!"

Other faces were peering into the pit now. I glanced over my shoulder and saw Pilazinool, 408b, Saul Shahmoon, and Jan. Incoherent with rage, Dr. Horkkk seized Pilazinool's leg and pointed at us while expostulating in what I suppose was the Thhhian language. Pilazinool tried to calm him.

Dr. Schein appeared, sized up the situation, and jumped down into the pit beside us.

The strange berserk frenzy that had overwhelmed us faded as soon as he arrived. Kelly put down her corer, Mirrik backed away from the globe, and I stood up, mopping off the sweat.

"What have we here?" Dr. Schein asked gently.

"An . . . artifact, sir . . ." I mumbled.

"Most unusual. Most unusual. Why the hurry though?"

"I don't know, sir. We got . . . carried away . . ."

"Well, we don't want to be carried away, do we? We need to follow orderly procedure, as Dr. Horkkk has been saying. I understand your enthusiasm, but nevertheless . . ." He frowned. "Who's charting the site?"

"Leroy Chang," I said.

"Where is he?"

I didn't know what to say, so I said nothing. I peered up at Jan and she smiled grimly. Her clothes were a little mussed, and she was soaked from her run in the rain, but she winked at me. As I say, Jan can take care of herself.

"Where is Professor Chang?" Dr. Schein repeated.

"He left the site about ten minutes ago," I said.

Dr. Schein looked puzzled, but shrugged the matter aside and picked up the chartbook. "Let's go, now," he said. "I'll supervise. Finish removing the globe . . . patiently."

With everyone watching us and Dr. Schein setting the pace, we completed the job in a more professional way. I felt guilty and embarrassed about that mad rush, and when Dr. Horkkk hopped into the pit for a closer look at the globe, I couldn't bear to face him. It took another half an hour to free the globe. Pilazinool, Dr. Schein, and Dr. Horkkk conferred about it in the pit; they all agreed it was some kind of High Ones machine and that it was by far the largest High Ones artifact ever found, but they had no more idea than I did of what it was. No one offered congratulations to me for having made the best discovery in this field since the finding of the first site. I didn't feel awfully proud of myself myself, considering the chimpo way I had carried on during the excavating work.

When the conference broke up, Mirrik reverently scooped the globe up on his tusks—it weighs about as much as a man, he says—and carried it to the lab. That was three hours ago. Dr. Schein, Dr. Horkkk, and Pilazinool have been in there all this time. With them is 408b; Saul Shahmoon has been going in and out. Each time he comes out he looks more excited than the time before, but he isn't saying a thing except that nothing definite has been learned yet.

Mirrik, Kelly, Steen Steen, and Leroy Chang have gone back to the dig. Leroy's face is a little bruised and he looks pretty sour about things. Jan and I were assigned to cleanup detail for the afternoon, she in her shack and I in mine.

That's a great reward for making a big find, isn't it?

.   .   .

Two hours later. The conference in the lab is still going on. I'd love to know what's up, but if they wanted apprentices in there, they'd invite us. Saul hasn't come out for a long time. The diggers are still at work, though they haven't found anything unusual. Kelly and Mirrik would dig all night, if we'd let them.

When I finished my cleanup I went across to talk to Jan.

She was less interested in discussing the strange ancient globe than she was in talking about Leroy Chang's uncouth behavior. I'd say that that's just like a girl, but I'd probably offend you, and besides I'm not sure I'm right.

"You saw him pawing me," Jan accused. "Why didn't you do something?"

"I didn't realize anything serious was going on."

"Serious? How much more serious could it have been? He practically had my clothes ripped off!"

"Good old Leroy. He sure knows how to coax a girl along."

"Very funny. Suppose he had raped me?"

"He didn't get very close to succeeding, did he?"

"No thanks to you. Down there in the pit digging like a madman, and me screaming for help."

I said, "You know, they say that rape isn't really possible unless the victim cooperates. I mean, all she has to do is defend herself, and if she's a girl of normal strength and her attacker isn't some kind of superman, she'll be able to fight him off. So when a rape happens, it's either because the girl is paralyzed with fear, or else because she secretly *wants* to be raped. Besides, I don't remember hearing you scream."

"I don't find your two-credit psychology very convincing," Jan said. "I don't know where you got that half-baked theory, but I can tell you it just isn't so. Like most men you don't have the first idea of what a woman's viewpoint is in such things."

"I suppose you've been raped a couple of times, so you know all about it."

"Can we change the subject? I can think of several hundred thousand subjects I'd rather discuss. And, no, I *haven't* been raped, and I mean to keep it that way, thank you."

"How did you discourage Leroy?"

"I hit him in the face. I didn't slap. I *hit*. Then I kicked."

"And he gave in. Which proves my theory that—"

"We were changing the subject."

"You were the first one who started talking about rape," I said.

"I don't want to hear that word again!"

"Right."

"And I still think it was foul of you to go on digging when Leroy began to—to attack me."

"I apologize. I got wrapped up in what I was doing."

"What *was* that thing, anyway?"

"I wish I knew," I said. "Shall we go over to the lab and see if they have any answers yet?"

"We'd better not. They don't want us there."

"You're probably right."

"I didn't mean to do so much cranking just now, Tom," she said. "It's just that Leroy scared me. And when nobody helped out—"

"Are you going to complain to Dr. Schein about him?"

She shook her head. "Leroy won't bother me again. There's no sense making a scandal out of it."

I admire Jan's attitude. I also may as well admit here that I admire Jan, too. So far in these letters I've been a little sketchy about that. Part of it is because I've only been slowly discovering how interesting a girl Jan really is, as well as being attractive in a physical way and all that. The other part is—well, forgive me, Lorie —I've always been uneasy about discussing my love life with you. Not because it embarrasses me to share such things with you, but because I'm afraid of hurting you.

There. It's out. Though maybe I'll blot this from the cube before I give it to you.

What I'm trying to say is that I don't want to touch on certain aspects of life that are closed to you on account of your condition. Like love and marriage and such. It's bad enough that I can lead an active physical life, going places and doing things, and you can't. But the whole social and emotional thing—dating, falling in love, taking out a temporary or a permanent marriage—you're cut off from that, and it makes me queasy to remind you of it by talking about my own adventures with girls, which are adequate and numerous enough, even if Mom thinks that at my age I ought to be more serious with somebody.

Isn't that great? How tactfully I explain to you why it is that I don't want to tell you certain things—even going out of my way to say that I don't like reminding you of matters which I proceed to remind you of. Swell. I will certainly blot this section of the cube as soon as I can figure out some more roundabout way of making it clear why I'm vague about such stuff.

Do you know why I'm more interested in Jan than I was at the beginning of this expedition?

No, wise one, it *isn't* because I'm getting hard up after all these weeks. It's because she told me last week that she's part non-human. Her grandmother was a Brolagonian.

Somehow that makes her more exotic. And more desirable than if she were an ordinary Swede. I've always been fascinated by the slightly unusual.

Brolagonians are humanoid aliens, you know, with

shiny gray skins and more toes and teeth than we have. They are one of about six or seven alien races in the galaxy that are able to mate successfully with Homo sapiens, owing to extremely close parallel evolution. It takes a lot of DNA manipulation and other genetic surgery to bring about a fertile mating, but it can be done, and it is done, despite the agitation of the League for Racial Purity and other reactionary groups.

Jan comes from a long line of diplomats. Her grandfather was our ambassador to Brolagon about sixty years ago and fell in love with a local girl. They married and had four children, and one of them was Jan's father. Who married a fellow Swede, but the Brolagonian genes are in the family for keeps.

Jan showed me some of the signs of her mixed blood. I blush to say I hadn't noticed any of them before.

"I have dark eyes," she said. "Instead of blue ones to go with the blonde hair. That isn't all that strange, really. But this is." She opened her sandals. She has six toes on each foot. Lovely toes, too. But six. "I also have forty teeth," she went on. "You can count them, if you don't believe me."

"I'll take it on faith," I said, as she gave me a dental yawn.

"My internal organs are also a little different. I don't have a large intestine. Take that on faith, too. The Brolagonian digestive process is different from yours. Also I have the Brolagonian birthmark, which is genetically dominant and is found on all Brolagonians and also all mixed-breeds. It's a very pretty birthmark, sort of geometrical and an interesting color, and if I ever get into trouble on a Brolagonian-controlled world all I have to do is show it, and it's as good as having a Brolagonian passport."

"Can I see it?" I asked.

"Don't be a lecher. It's in an embarrassing place."

"I have purely scientific curiosity. Besides, there aren't any embarrassing places, only embarrassed people. I didn't know you were so prudish."

"I'm not," said Jan. "But a girl's got to have *some* modesty."

"Why?"

"Beast!" she said, but she didn't sound very angry.

So I won't see her birthmark.

But I'm glad to know she has one. Call it snobbery, but I'm much taken by the news that Jan isn't entirely human. It seems so dull to confine yourself just to girls of your own species.

Of course, she's still desperately in love with Saul Shahmoon. Or says she is. I'm not sure she means it. Just as a scientific experiment, I kissed her. To see if a girl who is one-fourth Brolagonian kisses in an exotic way.

I didn't detect anything in the least Brolagonian about her kissing. However, she did seem remarkably enthusiastic, considering she keeps brooding over her unrequited love for Saul. Maybe she's losing patience with him. Maybe the rig-a-dig with Leroy this morning got her temporarily unhinged in the libido. Maybe—

I definitely am going to blot all this stuff before Lorie hears it. Right now I'm simply talking to myself, which is as good a way as any of sorting out one's feelings and emotions and things on a day when one has not only made a major scientific discovery but also fallen at least slightly in love with an unusual and very attractive female-type vidj. But I don't want to make things any tougher for Lorie by giving her these little sidelights on archaeological romance. How lousy it must be to be stuck in a hospital room for your whole life, with a million different monitoring instruments taped to your skin or hooked right into your nervous system, and knowing that you'll never walk, kiss or be kissed, go on a date, marry, have a family, anything! She's got her TP . . . but is it enough?

All this gets blotted.

.   .   .

Holy holocaust! Mirrik just galloped into view. He must have quit digging a couple of hours ago and gone off to his frostflower grove for some refreshment, because he's as looped as I've ever seen him. He came thundering by, gleaming with sweat and shouting what I suppose is Dinamonian poetry, and right now is doing a kind of war dance in front of the lab. I'd better get over there and steer him away before—

Oh, no!

He went *into* the lab! I can hear things crashing and smashing from here!

.   .   .

An hour later. Mirrik made quite a mess, but nobody cares about that now. Because it has also turned out that the machine I found is still in working order. It's a kind of movie projector.

Which is showing, right now, billion-year-old movies of the High Ones and their civilization.

six

September 6, 2375
Higby V

Mirrik has fool's luck. That caper yesterday afternoon should have finished him. Instead it made a hero out of him, in a zooby way, because everyone is now forgiving past sins.

It looked like disaster when he burst into the lab. The lab's a smallish bubble to start with, and it's set up for work, not to accommodate the leapings of a drunken Dinamonian. When I got there, Mirrik was trying to prance, which is a lost cause for a creature built like a rhinoceros, and with each clumsy bound he was knocking things off tables and breaking them. Dr. Horkkk had scrambled to the top of the bubble and was clinging there in terror. 408b was sitting on top of the computer; Dr. Schein had picked up one of the little lasers and was holding it like a dangerous weapon; and Pilazinool was hastily screwing his legs back in place and getting ready to defend himself. Mirrik loudly tried to explain that he had had a profound spiritual experience in the frostflower grove. "I have seen true wisdom!" he cried. "I have known revelation!"

He swung around and his rump knocked my High Ones globe to the floor.

It bounced. It gave off a sickening ringing sound.

And it turned on. Mirrik had loosened a jammed control.

We didn't know that, at first. We couldn't imagine *what* was happening. Mirrik's immense haunch was suddenly green instead of its usual blue, and figures appeared to be moving on his skin. That made no sense at all; but a moment later I began to see that he was serving as a screen for projected images, and that the images were coming out of the globe.

Then the field of projection widened to fill the entire lab. Strange, bizarre shapes flowed and coalesced along the walls. Nightmare scenes glistened in the air.

"Out of here!" Dr. Schein ordered. "Everyone out! Fast!"

The way he said it, I got the impression that something was going to explode. Mirrik must have thought so too, because he turned and fled at full gallop; the rest of us followed, all but Dr. Schein, Dr. Horkkk, and Pilazinool, who slammed the lab door shut behind us. Outside, we formed a stunned little group and tried to understand what had happened. Even Mirrik was sobered by it. He tottered off and plumped dismally to the ground, shaking his head and tapping his tusks.

An hour later we were allowed back into the lab.

"Here he is," Dr. Schein called out, as I entered. "The discoverer himself!" Then Mirrik came in, looking around a little sheepishly. "And here's the one who switched it on!"

So at last I was getting a little credit. And was forgiven, I guess, for the breathless way I got the globe out of the ground. Mirrik, too, had won amnesty for his chimpo behavior. At a time like this, who could hold grudges?

The globe was sitting on the workbench in the part of the lab where they had stacked up the inscription nodes. It was perfectly round, and looked more like some kind of sculpture than a machine, except for the control dials on one side. In the smooth parts between the raised strips and the buttons and knobs I could see my own reflection, with my face drawn out and narrowed like something in a funhouse mirror.

Dr. Schein had summoned everybody to the viewing. He had a This-Is-Something-BIG look on his face; fussy little Dr. Horkkk seemed positively aglow. Pilazinool had not only taken himself apart, as he usually did in moments of stress, but had absentmindedly put himself back together the wrong way, with his left hand on his right arm, and so on. It took me a moment to figure out why he looked so strange.

408b ambled forward at a signal from Dr. Schein. Its eyes were blinking rapidly in groups of three, which meant that things must really have been fissioning inside the Bellatrician's brain. It nodded jerkily, opened and closed its beak a few times, and finally said, "I have very little to explain, since I understand very little. The device you see before you functions as a projector but has no visible lenses or optical outlets. Nor does it require a screen for reception of its image. We also are unaware of its power source. It is controlled by this lever"—it tapped a little stud—"which we discovered only through accident. Darken the room, please." 408b picked up a movie camera and used several of its tentacles to focus and start it. "Since we do not know how long the globe will continue to function, nor whether we will be able to induce it to repeat any of the scenes it plays for us, we are making a complete film record each time we use it."

It touched the stud.

Greenish light blossomed from the globe. The zone of light expanded until it became a sphere more than twenty meters in diameter, practically filling our section of the lab. Suddenly we saw figures moving along the surface of the sphere of light.

High Ones.

What we were getting was a 360-degree movie, with ourselves inside the projection field. The globe was showing us five or six different sequences, each blurring imperceptibly into its neighbor. As we turned, certain sequences vanished and were replaced by others; but a few remained constant. It was a struggle to take in anything, because so much was going on. In the first few minutes I went spinning round and round in my place, trying to scan everything at once, and unhappy because one scene was vanishing even while I was trying to figure out what another one was all about. I didn't envy the scholars who would have to make sense out of all this. At least there was a camera with a fisheye lens stationed right next to the globe, filming the whole giboo in all 360 degrees. The only way to deal with an information glut, you know, is to make a record of all incoming data and then cope with each item, bit by bit, at your own data-handling speed.

After a little while I stopped rotating and concentrated on viewing each sequence at length, despite the frustration of having to miss all the rest of what was going on. I'll try to describe some of the pictures I saw.

One scene took place in a city of the High Ones. I think so, anyhow. I saw figures moving around, the dome-headed, six-limbed humanoids familiar to us from the plaque designs. Their skins were a deep, rich green in color and were covered by shining overlapping scales, hinting at some kind of reptilian ancestry, perhaps. They glided rather than walked, seemed almost to float; I can't explain why they looked so graceful.

Their city consisted of sky-high pillars set perhaps fifty meters apart—I had no way of judging scale. High overhead, a kind of netting was strung to connect the tops of all the pillars. Buildings dangled from the netting like spiders from a spiderweb, each swaying gently at the end of a long cable, each at a different distance from the web above and each far from the ground. These suspended buildings mainly had a teardrop shape, although there were spherical, octagonal, and cubical ones too. Smaller cables provided transport from one dangling building to another; the air was full of High Ones riding up, down, or sideways, clinging to cables that appeared to move of their own will. A golden-green sunlight filtered through the top of the web, giving everything an undersea look. As I watched, night came; and suddenly the light of a thousand stars blazed down, and the buildings themselves began to move, sliding upward or downward on their cables, while High Ones in great numbers passed from one to another. I have seen alien scenes, Lorie, but nothing so alien as this. Those huge, graceful beings (somehow I think of them as much bigger than humans), those dangling houses, that eerie daylight and that dazzling starlight, all blended into something immensely strange.

The camera angles added to the effect. I would have thought that just about every way of filming a scene has already been used in the four centuries or so since Edison rigged up his first movie camera. But whoever had taken this billion-year-old flick had not seen things remotely the way a modern cameraman would; and so we had a constantly shifting viewpoint, now from above, now from underneath, now from within, the camera drifting around that weird city so freely that I had to grab the edge of the lab bench to keep from falling over in dizziness.

For a long while I watched as though in a dream as these beings went about their unimaginable business, gliding up and down on their cables, bowing to one another, gracefully touching hands, exchanging gifts (I saw some inscription nodes being handed out), and engaging in conversations that I could not hear, for there was no sound accompanying the projection. Then I turned to face the next sequence.

It showed a scene inside one of the dangling houses: a large red-lit room whose walls appeared covered with a living substance, something soft and rippling that swelled and shrank in an unpredictable cycle, now puffing up and becoming tight as a drumhead, now deflating, now writhing like sheets of flesh.

There were nine High Ones in the room. Two, clutching cables mounted in the ceiling, were lost in trances, or, for all I could tell, were dead and stuffed. (The funeral customs of alien races defy all comprehension. So do the funeral customs of non-alien races. Can you explain to me the virtue of putting dead people in a box and burying the box in the ground?) Three of the High Ones stood in a far corner, taking part in what might have been a quaint folk dance or perhaps some kind of sex: they had formed a circle, facing inward, with their arms interlaced and their heads pressed cheek-to-cheek, and they were sliding around and around and around in a slow, determined way. You figure it out. Another High One was crouched over a miniature model of a globe much like the one that was entertaining us; it was projecting a tiny image, but we weren't able to see it clearly. The remaining three High Ones sat in a pit in the floor, passing a flask of some colored fluid back and forth, and now and then dipping the tips of their fingers into it.

The adjoining sequence showed a building under construction. First a cable descended from the webwork. Then machines at ground level sent spurts of—plastic?—into the air. Midway between ground and web the spurted stuff collected around the cable as if pulled to it by a magnetic field, and shaped itself into a neat eight-sided structure. Everything was done automatically, and it took about six minutes.

The fourth sequence was a purely abstract pattern, a

coiling and uncoiling of green and red shapes that was so unsettling and disturbing that I don't feel like talking about it.

The fifth sequence revealed an empty landscape, no trees, no grass, ice-covered boulders scattered about, sky copper-red, ground iron-gray, the sun pale and feeble. In the middle distance was another group of three High Ones, heads inward, arms interlaced, cheeks touching, doing that same slow dance.

The sixth sequence presented the interior of some kind of cave whose walls were encrusted with huge uncut gems, great glistening crystals of a hundred different kinds. The camera peered through the floor of the cave, which appeared to be made of glass, and revealed colossal machines throbbing and hammering in an underground chamber: huge green pistons pumping endlessly, sleek black conveyor belts, spinning turbines. High Ones wearing yellow belts (the only clothing I saw on any of them) walked down the aisles between these devices, pausing occasionally to examine control panels.

I had come full circle, for the adjoining sequence was the city scene again, not much changed. But the room with the nine High Ones had vanished, and now I saw a close-up shot of a single High One who held an inscription node in his hands. The camera zoomed in on the inscription and lingered there a long while, long enough for the inscription to change several times.

The sequence next to this no longer showed the construction project; now it depicted—

But why go on? For a full hour I watched these

scenes, all of them fascinating, all of them bewildering. I could continue multiplying mysteries by listing everything, but you must have the idea by now of how remote and strange these people were, how advanced their civilization, how little we comprehend them.

Curious thing. The usual effect of archaeology is to discover kinships with the ancients. "How very much like ourselves the early Egyptians were!" an Egyptologist will say. "Lying, cheating, fixing elections, dodging the draft, all our own special little sins, existed back then too! Even as we, the subjects of Pharaoh had foibles and ambitions, hopes and dreams," etcetera, etcetera. Substitute Sumerians for Egyptians, or Cro-Magnon cave painters for Sumerians, and you will still find the experts telling you that the more closely we get to know them, the clearer it is that these figures out of the remote past were Just Plain Folks.

Zit! Not the case at all with the High Ones! This globe I found told us a million times as much about them as we knew before: the way they looked and moved, the shape of their cities, something of their customs. And they don't seem like Just Plain Folks at all. They seem tremendously alien, far stranger than Shilamakka or Dinamonians or Thhhians or any of the alien beings we encounter in our own lives. We may have difficulty understanding Dinamonian theology or the Shilamakkan craze for replacing perfectly good limbs with machinery, but we can still get along with them on a business basis. I don't think we could ever have gotten along with the High Ones, even if they weren't separated from us by a billion-year gap. Not only because of their immense technological superiority, either. They way they *think* would always be unintelligible.

Consider the cultures of Earth before communications satellites and rocket transport helped everybody to live just like everybody else. Consider the world-outlooks of Eskimos, Polynesians, Bedouins, Belgian businessmen, Pueblo Indians, and Tibetans. Not a whole lot in common there. Pretty alien to one another, matter of fact, and *all native to the same planet*. Okay, eventually they all died out or became smoodged together into "Earthmen," but now we were part of a galaxy full of other intelligent species, each one with its own various cultures, and each one different from us . . . and so on. Huge gulfs between peoples of the same world, and huger gulfs between peoples of different worlds, yet all these gulfs were bridgeable.

The hugest gulf of all seems to be the one between us and the High Ones. Forget my romantic ideas about finding them still alive somewhere. I don't want to find them any more. I think it would be pretty frightening if we did.

.   .   .

After an hour of viewing the globe, 408b shut it off and we had a Discussion. The eleven of us sat around trying to interpret what we had just seen. Jan carefully positioned herself as far from Leroy Chang as she could get, but Leroy seemed to be going out of his way not to look at her. He seemed twitchy and ill at ease, more so than usual; I guess he was scared that Jan was going to rise up and denounce him as a rapist. A bungling rapist, at that. (Question: Is a man more loathsome if he succeeds in Having His Way with a woman, or if he's such a spineless vidj that he botches the job? Don't bother answering.)

Dr. Schein acted as chairman. He said, "It's apparent that the whole scope of High Ones archaeology has changed overnight. For the first time we know something of what their living culture was like, as a result of Tom Rice's fine discovery."

I glowed nicely and nodded to acknowledge the cheers of a multitude of admirers.

Dr. Horkkk dampened my furnace a little by saying crisply, "Let it be noted that as a result of careless excavation technique this miraculous artifact nearly was destroyed."

I looked at the floor in shame and counted my toes for lack of anything else to do. Dr. Horkkk tacked on a few more criticisms in his neat Teutonic way and I tried to shrink out of sight. Jan, who was sitting next to me, whispered, "Don't let him get you quonked. You *did* find it. And you *didn't* damage it." I should have added that Jan had chosen to sit next to me instead of Saul Shahmoon. Interesting. Is she trying to awaken his slumbering jealousies, or do Jan and I have something going?

When Dr. Horkkk finished flaying me, 408b said, "It is questionable that this instrument represents a view of the living culture of these beings. Perhaps it is an entertainment device, providing pure fantasy."

"Good point," said Dr. Schein. "But I don't go for it."

Pilazinool took off one hand and waved it in the

other to get the floor. The mechanical man said, "On the basis of a quick analysis, I too doubt that 408b is correct. I feel that we've got an authentic look at High Ones life, here. I can't say what purpose this globe was meant to serve, but I do believe that those were genuine scenes of daily life, as Dr. Schein suggests."

Dr. Schein beamed. 408b folded his tentacles in irritation. Mirrik, Saul Shahmoon, and Kelly offered opinions, more or less simultaneously. I didn't have the slice to open my glapper after the things Dr. Horkkk had said about me, but privately I agreed with Pilazinool and Dr. Schein.

"The question is," Dr. Schein said, "should we ship the globe back to Galaxy Central for detailed study of the content of its images, or should we keep it here to guide us in the remaining period of our excavations?"

"Keep it here," said Pilazinool.

"Send it to Galaxy Central," said Dr. Horkkk.

We went around on that for a while. It developed that Dr. Horkkk was so enthralled with the globe that he proposed calling the expedition off at this point, heading back toward civilization, and devoting all our efforts to trying to learn things from the projected scenes. Leroy Chang seconded the motion. I guess Leroy is looking for any excuse to get off Higby V after that fiasco with Jan.

Steen Steen said, "That seems hasty. Why leave now, when we may be on the verge of even more amazing discoveries?"

First sensible thing I ever heard him/her say.

Dr. Horkkk replied, "As long as we stay here with the globe, we run the risk that it may be lost or destroyed. It's our duty to convey it safely to some more settled world."

Dr. Schein, who in his mild way can be murderous, smiled sweetly at his Thhhian rival and said, "Perhaps, Dr. Horkkk, you and Professor Chang would be willing to detach yourselves from the expedition and take the globe to a safer planet, while the rest of us proceed with the work?"

Dr. Horkkk made a gargling sound. He wasn't pleased by that maneuver.

In the end, when all the verbal knifeplay was over, a reasonable decision emerged. All of us, *and* the globe, will remain on Higby V while we complete our scheduled period of excavation work. For safety's sake, though, we'll make several copies of the films of the globe's projections and ship them out to civilization aboard the monthly transport packets. Jan and I were given the assignment of writing up a press release about the globe which is to be sent out via the TP communications network as soon as possible. We're supposed to write the release tonight.

The work schedule is going to be revised somewhat. Pilazinool, 408b, and Dr. Horkkk will be relieved of all supervisory work at the excavation and instead will devote themselves pretty much full time to playing the globe and puzzling over the meaning of the scenes it shows. The hope is to get some clue that will lead us to other important discoveries. This means that the burden of overseeing the digging will fall to Dr. Schein and Leroy Chang, since Saul will be busy classifying artifacts in the lab, and that most of the actual grubbing in the pit will be done by our two specialized

diggers, Mirrik and Kelly, and by the three apprentices, Steen, Jan, and yours cordially.

Dinnertime now. Nasty rain coming down.

I still feel dazed by the things the globe projected.
Those dangling buildings . . . the weird customs . . .
above all, just seeing the faces of the High Ones. Did I
mention their eyes? Three of them, side by side. Cold.
Glittering. They look at you out of those projected
images and you want to crawl into the ground. That
look of chilly intelligence . . . of having lived a hundred thousand years. It's terrifying to meet a High
One's stare, coming at you across so much time. What
kind of race was this? Where did they learn the skills
that let them grow so great before all the other races of
the galaxy had begun to evolve? How were they able to
keep their civilization intact for all those hundreds of
millions of years? (Hundreds of *millions* of years!
Those long-ago Egyptians and Cro-Magnons happened
just an eye-blink back, on a scale like that!)

So much for deep philosophical thoughts. Your
handsome and profound brother is hungry. Off for
now.

.   .   .

Bedtime, five hours later, same night.

Jan and I spent a couple of hours after dinner writing our press release. Actually she wrote the whole
thing, though I'm supposed to have verbal skills and so
on. I fooled around doing a couple of trial drafts and
scrapped them; then she got to work and knocked off a
professional-sounding statement with the greatest of
ease. This girl has much orbital velocity. Tomorrow

morning we go into town to give the release to the TP people, and I trust that that lady dog Marge Hotchkiss will be off duty.

Everybody else spent the evening in the lab. Jan and I went over there when we were finished. Chess is obsolete here; as of today, the only evening activity is going to be watching the scenes that come out of that globe. There were some new ones tonight, as baffling as the earlier ones. The thing seems to have an infinite number of reels, or whatever, inside it. I hope we don't burn it out.

seven

September 10, 2375
Higby V

Jan and I almost didn't make it into town to deliver
the press release. Some dumb clump had forgotten to
recharge the battery of the electric runabout we use for
commuting between town and the site. We were still
twelve kilometers from town when the engine gave a
soft sighing sound and zapped out. I opened the hood
and tried to show masculine competence, but there
wasn't a thing I could do, and we both knew it. Jan
called to me, "The battery's dead. Don't waste time
playing with the engine."

"What do we do now? Walk the rest of the way?"

"It's starting to rain," she said. "What a lovely surprise!"

"Let's wait. Maybe somebody'll come along."

We waited for half an hour, all alone together in the
middle of emptiness. I took no advantage of my great

opportunity to slip in a little biology. For one thing, the endless gray downpour that is this planet's characteristic weather has definitely dismalized my passions. For another, even if I had happened to be in the mood, I wouldn't have wanted to get involved in anything at the risk of failing to notice a passing car. Traffic isn't so heavy on that road that stranded wayfarers can afford to let a lot of potential rescuers go by. Most important, though, was this strange and old-fashioned attitude that suddenly came over me: that it would be bad form to launch a possibly quite serious romance in a stalled runabout on a muddy road. Not that Higby V offers more luxurious surroundings anywhere, but I rebelled against the sordidness of it all. I can be quite perverse sometimes. I think you know that.

So instead of leaping lasciviously at each other, we sat chastely side by side and talked. It occurs to me now that Jan may not have shared my sudden puritanism, but it's too late to do anything about that. Mostly what we talked about was how we happened to go in for archaeology. She asked me, and I said, "It's because I hate to think that anything goes to waste. I mean, that anything that was ever important or valuable or precious to somebody is just buried and forgotten about. I want to salvage all those things and let them be important to somebody again . . . so they won't feel neglected."

And I told her the Lost Statuette Story.

Do you remember, Lorie? How could you have forgotten? We were six years old. Dad had been on a planet whose name I can't recall, in the epsilon Eridani system, setting up one of his real-estate deals, and he brought back two little native statuettes as toys for us, one for you, one for me. They were images of pet animals of that planet, made out of some kind of porcelain extremely smooth and voluptuous to the touch, so that once you began fingering it, you didn't want to stop. You kept your statuette next to your bed at the hospital, and I kept mine in my pocket except when I slept, and then it sat on the night table so I could reach out for it in the night. And I loved that little porcelain animal more than anything else I owned, and then one day Dad took me to watch them constructing a new building he was putting up in Alaska, and I was on this balcony, looking down into the foundation site, with the statuette in my hands, and I sneezed or something and it fell into the site. I started to scream, and told Dad to get it back for me, but the construction machines were too fast; they poured tons of concrete into that hole in the next five minutes. "Make them dig it up!" I said to Dad. "You own the building! You can make them! I want it back!" He laughed and said it would cost thousands of credits to look for my toy under the concrete, and did I want him to waste that much money? Besides, he said, a million years from now archaeologists would come there and explore the ruins of the building and find my toy, and put it in a museum. I didn't know what an archaeologist was, and I didn't want the statuette dug up a million years from now, I wanted it right that minute, and I threw such a howling tantrum that they had to take me away and give me something to calm me down. And when you heard what had happened, you said, "Well, if Tom doesn't have his statue, I don't want to have mine either," and you told your nurse to give it away to some other little girl, and she did. Which was a typically subtle and sensitive Lorie-type thing to do, since I was madly jealous that you still had your toy and I had lost mine. I suppose an ordinary good-hearted sister would just have given her own toy to her brother, but you never did things the ordinary way, and what you did was just right, because I wouldn't have been satisfied with a substitute for what I had lost, but your not having one either somehow took the sting out of the whole incident.

Later I found out what archaeologists were. And started going to museums to see the things they had dug up, including plenty of toys lost by other little boys five or ten or fifty thousand years ago. And it struck me: how sad it is that these things were lost and had no one to love them and care for them. And how fine it is that somebody takes the trouble to find them again, after all those years. Still later I thought: how sad it is that whole civilizations are lost, whole slabs of the past, kings and poets and artists, customs and religions and sculptures and kitchen utensils and tools, and how fine it is that somebody takes the trouble to find them again, after all those years. Then I made up my mind that I was going to be one of the finders. Which horrified Our Father, naturally, since he had already decided I was going to be a real-estate tycoon just like himself. "Archaeology? What kind of thing is this archaeology for someone like you? I've got an *empire* waiting for you, Tom!" I said I was more interested in empires that don't exist any more. I couldn't really tell him that at the bottom of everything was a toy animal from epsilon Eridani.

As I finished, Jan said, "When you dug up the globe the other day—that wonderful toy—was it anything like finding your lost statuette again?"

"Yes. Very much. I found a whole world again, Jan. That's what this is all about."

"Suppose your father *had* stopped the construction machinery and ordered his men to dig your toy out of the new concrete? Do you think you'd be on Higby V today?"

"I think I'd be a junior-grade real-estate tycoon today," I said, and I believe it's true.

Then I asked Jan why she had become an archaeologist. Her answer was a little disappointing. She didn't dredge up any dark episodes out of her childhood. "Because it's interesting," she said. "That's all. The idea of finding out what the past was like is very interesting to me."

Well, of course, that isn't any answer at all. We know that archaeologists find archaeology interesting; the real problem is *why* they do. I think the answer is that all of us are looking for some kind of lost toy. We are fighting that force in the universe that nudges everything toward chaos. I mean that we are at war with time; we are enemies of entropy; we seek to snatch back those things that have been taken from us by the years—the childhood toys, the friends and relatives who are gone, the events of the past—everything, we struggle to recapture everything, back to the beginning of creation, out of this need not to let anything slip away. Forgive the philosophizing. I don't know if Jan or anybody else here would agree with me, and I don't want to delve. Maybe some of them would say that for them it's just a job, or a means toward prestige, or a way of passing time, who knows? I really do think that beneath those reasons there has to be something more complicated.

The trouble with a serious, intense discussion, I find, is that it ultimately becomes a little awkward to continue when the people doing the talking don't know each other too well. In an earnest way we made a stab at talking about Dad's hostility to my going into archaeology, and likesuch topics, but the atmosphere of earnestness started depressing us. I had to do something. Either make a pass at Jan, which somehow seemed less appropriate than ever after all this solemn palaver, or else get out and pretend I could do something about starting the engine. I got out.

Jan said, "Why try to look chivalrous? You know there's absolutely nothing you can do to fix it. Unless you can rub your fingers together and spurt some wattage into the battery."

I grinned sickly at her as I stood in the rain. "We might sit here all week," I said.

"So? They'll send out a rescue party. Come back inside."

I did, and a minute later a military truck appeared. Three soldiers were in it; they stopped when they saw we were stalled, became very attentive indeed when they got a good look at Jan (girls of her contours are extremely rare on this miserable outpost of the Terran Empire), and lewdly suggested that she ride to town with them while I stayed behind to guard the runabout. They looked hurt when Jan vetoed the idea. I drew sour looks of undisguised envy from them; I guess they figured Jan and I had been making feverish love while awaiting help. Let them stew.

They gave us a ride to town, finally.

Sour looks were in style there, too. The first place we went was the communications office, and naturally the TP on duty was Marge Hotchkiss Herself, that radioactively charming seductress. She slouched over to the counter and said, "Yeah? What now?"

"We have a press release to send out. For relay to the nearest Galactic News Service TP pickup."

"Well, okay." She consulted a ratebook. "Five hundred credits, thumb to the plate."

I stared at the computer input on her desk. "I'm not authorized to make charges here."

"You *are* a feeb, aren't you? Why didn't they send someone whose thumbprint is registered? '

"GNS will accept a collect call from us," I explained. "It's already been arranged."

Hotchkiss grew more sullen. "How do *I* know?"

"But—"

"You want me to go to the trouble of setting up a hookup just to find out if they'll take a collect from you. Only what if they say no? I've wasted a shot of TP energy. I'm no goddam machine, sonny. You want to make a call, you pay for it."

And she sneered. Like something out of medieval melodrama. I've never been sneered at before. She was an expert sneerer, too. Must have had lots of practice.

Jan was standing to one side during this exchange, obviously sizzling, but unwilling to cut in. This was my show. I'd look pretty spineless if I couldn't even get the local TP operator to accept a collect call. I wanted to do something virile and forceful, like throw Marge Hotchkiss through the wall. I began to rage and bluster. I told her that my sister was a TP supervisor and would have her fired, a lie for which I hope to be forgiven. I demanded to see her superior. I threatened to report her to the network coordinator. The louder I yelled, the more curdled the Hotchkiss expression became, and the more defiant she got. "You can take your collect call," she said, "and—"

"Wait a moment," Jan said sweetly, at last. "According to the section of the Public Utilities Act of 2322 that governs the operations of the TP network, it's illegal for any representative of the communications net to refuse to accept a collect call. The TP operative is not permitted to exercise independent judgment as to whether such a call will be ultimately accepted, but must undertake to inquire of the party called as to whether the call will be received."

Marge Hotchkiss looked sick.

"What are you, a company spy?" she snapped. "All right, I'll see if GNS will accept the call."

Hotchkiss slipped into the TP trance and reached out toward the nearest pickup point of the news service, which I guess was about twenty light-years away. (You'd know that better than I, Lorie.) After a moment she returned her attention to us and said, still sullen, "Let's have that blenking message of yours."

I handed it over. Hotchkiss scanned it and began to relay it to the GNS operator. I began to wonder whether she might just garble it out of general bitchiness, and, if so, what protection we had against such sabotage. Jan must have thought the same thing, because when Hotchkiss was finished, Jan said, "Thank you very much. We'd like a confirming playback, of course."

Why didn't I think of that?

Hotchkiss glared demonically, but—half afraid that Jan really was a company spy checking up on her efficiency—she dutifully requested a playback of the message from her TP counterpart out yonder, wrote it down as it came in, and handed it to us for comparison. It checked out with the original down to the last comma.

"Very good," Jan said. "Thank you *so* much!"

Outside the TP office I asked her how she had known that stuff about the Public Utilities Act of 2322, and so forth. "Don't tell me you're a refugee from the TP network," I said.

"Oh, no! I don't have a TP molecule in me, Tom. But I once watched my father get into a similar mess with a network girl, and I remembered how he got out of it."

"Clever."

"Why are all these TP people so slicy, though? Especially the females. They seem to be doing you a tremendous favor just to put your calls through. I guess they must really have contempt for us poor zoobs who don't have their powers, and are forced to use mere words to communicate."

"They aren't all slicy," I said. "My sister isn't. Lorie's very patient with everybody. Lorie's a saint, in fact."

"If she is, she's the first TP girl I've ever heard of

who shows any civility. How come I never draw some-one like that when *I* have to make a call?"

"Lorie doesn't take calls from the public," I said. "On account of she's confined to her hospital room all the time. She's strictly pickup and relay."

"It figures. They've probably got all the decent human beings working relay, and all the slicy howlers manning the public offices. I'd like to meet your sister some day."

"Maybe you will."

"Does she look much like you?"

"Not really. She's shorter and softer and rounder in some places. Also she doesn't need to shave."

"Dodo! I mean, aside from her being a girl!"

"They say we look a lot alike, especially for fraternal twins," I said. "It's hard for me to judge that. She's quieter than I am, and has a different kind of sense of humor. I mean, she's likely not to say anything for half an hour or so, just listening to the other people in her room, and then she'll come out with something in a very soft voice, so that you have to strain your ears to hear it, and it'll be something absolutely devastating, something that manages to be funny and true all at once. She can really fuse a person sometimes, with two or three well-chosen words."

"You must miss her very much."

"This is the longest I've ever gone without speaking with her. I've always tried to share all my experiences with her—whatever I do, wherever I go. But here—this far away—"

"You could call her."

"Via Smiling Marge?" I shook my head. "I don't

want to contaminate Lorie's mind by unnecessary contact with that species of microorganism. Besides, it takes mucho stash.''

"Isn't your father rich?"

"My father is. I'm not. He keeps his thumb in his own pocket."

"Oh."

"I'm piling up message cubes for Lorie, telling her the whole story. When I get back to Earth I'll let her play them back in sequence, two years of letters all at once."

"So that's who you've been writing to!"

"You've noticed?"

"Half the time lately when I've gone looking for you, you've been off by yourself talking into a message cube," Jan said.

Interesting. That she would go looking for me.

For strategic purposes I said, "Of course, those cubes haven't *all* been for Lorie. I mean, you understand, not that I have any ties back on Earth of a formal kind, but there are a couple of girls who I think are interested in my adventures in the outer galaxy, and—"

"Certainly," Jan said. "It's thoughtful of you to keep them in mind when you're so far away."

Her tone was absolutely neutral. I detected no tinge of the jealousy that I was clumsily trying to arouse, and instantly I regretted the whole stupid adolescent ploy. Either Jan couldn't care less about my supposed Earthside amours (which of course I had invented on the spot, since the only letters I'm writing are to you) or else, even worse, she had seen through the maneuver and wasn't awed by my pretensions to galactic playboyhood. I wished she'd tell me about some lad far away who made *her* aorta palpitate, just by way of hurling back the challenge, but she didn't even do that. Her cool brown Brolagonian eyes offered me no information whatever. I was dealing with a girl with a ten-generation heritage of professional diplomacy. The only secrets she gives away are those she wants to give away.

We picked up a new battery for the runabout and ran a couple of other errands in town. Then Jan inveigled an off-duty soldier to drive us out to the place where we had abandoned the runabout. Her technique was neat: she had me lurk in the background until the ride was arranged; then I stepped forward, and there wasn't a thing her victim could do about it except look disgruntled. By way of consolation Jan sat snuggled up close to him in the front seat on the way out. I hope that gruntled him a little.

This is a very capable girl. In many ways.

.   .   .

For the past several days we've been getting a new sequence out of the globe. It must be an important one, because it recurs every few hours, and on occasion it has simultaneously been projected on two of the 60-degree segments into which the circular viewing field is usually divided. No other scene has so far appeared in duplicate that way.

It looks like a teaser sequence for a space-opera video show. This is how it goes:

First we see a wide-angle view of a galaxy, perhaps ours, with constellations strewn across a dark background. Camera pans back and forth to give us a dizzying view at least a thousand parsecs wide. Then we zoom forward for a close-up of one patch of sky. Supply the music yourself: a high screechy crescendo. *Suspense!* Now we see about ten stars: a binary, a red giant, a white dwarf, a couple of main-sequence yellow stars, two Class O and B blazers, the whole family straight out of the Hertzsprung-Russell diagram.

We head toward the white dwarf, and now it is very clear that the camera is mounted in the nose of a starship on which we are the passengers. The music adds something low and ominous and throbbing, at about thirty cycles. *Mystery!* The white dwarf has five planets. It looks like we're making for the fourth planet, which moves in an orbit pretty far away from number three. But no: there is a course correction and we turn our snout toward a region between the orbits of planets three and four.

Suddenly an asteroid emerges from nowhere and swims past our point of view from left to right. The music gives a sharp stab to underline the unexpectedness of it. *The unknown!* We realize that an asteroid belt lies between the third and fourth planets; the void is littered with all sorts of cosmic debris, just as it is between Mars and Jupiter. Remnants of a shattered planet, maybe. We are in orbit around a large, knobby asteroid whose jagged mountains gleam a dull pink in the faint light from the distant dwarf sun. We're landing, now, on a broad pockmarked plain.

Shift of viewpoint. Camera is no longer in nose of ship; now it's a couple of hundred meters away, looking *at* ship. Which is standing upright on its tail like any modern vessel, but otherwise is a thoroughly alien job. No visible sign of propulsion devices. No attempt at streamlining. The ship is squat, copper-colored, unattractive. Along its flanks are inscriptions in large High Ones hieroglyphics similar to those on the inscription nodes, except that here the lettering doesn't shift around at random.

Hatches open high up on the ship. Cables emerge and dangle. High Ones descend to the ground.

They are wearing masks of some sort; obviously the atmosphere on this asteroid doesn't agree with them, assuming there's an atmosphere at all, which doesn't look likely. They move about in their strange gliding way, now and then fluttering their arms in graceful signals to one another. About a dozen of them come from the ship. Then a hatch much lower on the ship's side rolls open and a ramp juts forth. Down the ramp come six massive robots. They are built to the same four-arm-two-leg-domed-head design as the High Ones themselves, but there is no mistaking their artificial nature. Instead of eyes, they have a single glowing vision panel running entirely around the upper part of the head. Their arms have various mechanical attachments specialized for digging, grasping, etcetera. (408b has suggested that these six are simply High Ones surgically transformed into machines, as Shilamakka are today. But Pilazinool, who after all *is* a Shilamakka, doesn't think so. It's anybody's guess. I think they're robots.)

The High Ones contingent leads the robots, single file, across the plain to a low hill. A signal is given and abruptly the robot in front points an arm at the hill, and flame sprouts, and the rock begins to melt and run off in puddles. The robot keeps this laser attachment, or whatever it is, running until a goodly-sized cave has been carved in the hillside. Then the other robots move in, clearing away the debris, trimming things up. When they finish (five minutes later, in the globe's version) there is a neat six-sided room within the hill. The camera tracks right inside to show the robots at work, gently melting the rock walls with gadgets mounted on their leftmost arms, to put a nice glaze over the surface. Then they install a heavy metal door on a colossal hinge. They carry an assortment of machinery into the room and arrange it along the back walls. Finally one of the robots sits down in the middle of the floor, and the door swings shut. They seal it, with the robot inside. Everybody returns to the ship. They get in, the robots going up the ramp, the High Ones hauled up on the cables.

The ship blasts off. End of sequence.

Why did the High Ones leave the robot marooned in the cave on that dismal asteroid? As punishment? That seems like a lot of trouble and bother. To watch for enemies? Why?

And why does the scene show up so often when we use the globe? That in itself shows that there was some special significance in building the rock vault and leaving the robot in it. But what?

Meanwhile we keep digging and have settled into a daily routine. Since my discovery of the globe nothing of special interest has come to light. Mirrik and Kelly are tireless, though. They chip away at the site, we clear it, Saul processes thousands of artifacts. On the basis of hieroglyphic styles, potassium-argon tests, and other evidence, he has now dated our site to 925,000,-000 years ago, with a probable error of 50,000,000 years in either direction. That's a pretty big margin for error. I still like to think of the place as having been occupied a round billion years ago. There's something boomy and majestic about the word "billion." I say it with a good explosion on the *b*. I feel sorry for the poor archaeologist chaps who can claim only a pitiful few thousand years of antiquity for *their* sites.

*B*illion. *B*illion. One thousand million and seven years ago, the High Ones brought forth upon this planet—

I still wish I knew what that rock-vault scene was all about.

.   .   .

Your brother has distinguished himself again, this time by a brainstorm. When I got the idea, it sounded absolutely chimpo to me, but I worked up the courage to try it on Jan, who was thrilled and insisted I tell everybody about it at that evening's discussion session. Which I did, although as I heard the sound of my own voice uttering the first few words of my wild notion, I began to feel like a tightrope performer with defective antigravs, bravely striding out over nothing at all and about to take a plunge.

There was no turning back, though.

Everybody stared intently at me as I said, "Let's assume, just for the sake of argument, that the High Ones left that robot sealed in the vault and never came back for it. On an airless and waterless asteroid, a metal object such as a robot, built with High Ones technology, might very well last a billion years without eroding away or suffering other harm. This globe here is our proof that that's possible. Therefore it's at least theoretically conceivable that the robot is still sitting behind that thick door, as good as new."

People began to frown, to nod, to fidget. I felt myself tumbling into an abyss. Such nonsense I was spouting! In front of Dr. Schein, Dr. Horkkk, all these experienced archaeologists!

Helpless, I went on.

"The question is, can we find the asteroid where the vault is located? I think we can. We have certain clues. The opening shot of the sequence gives us a broad pan shot of at least a thousand parsecs of space. The constellations shown, naturally, are a billion years old and don't have that configuration any more, nor do we have any idea which sector of space was being photographed. Even so, I think any good observatory could provide us with computer simulations of various regions of our galaxy as they looked a billion years ago. Perhaps we could get a hundred such simulations, spaced two or three million years apart, to cover possible errors in our dating of the globe.

"This may locate the part of the galaxy shown in that opening shot. Next we zero in on our close-up: that little group of stars, the red giant, the binary, the yellow stars, the blue-white ones. Of course, a billion years is a long time even in stellar evolution. I imagine that those hot O-type stars cooled a long time ago, that the red giant may be a white dwarf by now, and that the white dwarf may have burned out altogether. It's also possible that these stars may have had very different velocities and are no longer anywhere near one another in space. Nevertheless, it's not all that tricky for an astronomical computer to find some of the key members of that group, track them backward on their paths, and come up with a simulation of where they were a billion years ago. With a certain amount of luck we'll find the white dwarf still associated with some members of the group. An expedition can go there and hunt for the asteroid, and then it can't be too much of a problem to find . . . the vault . . . the robot . . ."

I ran out of juice. My idea sounded so absurd to me that I couldn't go on. I sank limply into my seat and waited for the derisive hooting to begin.

"Brilliant!" Dr. Horkkk cried. Dr. Horkkk, no less.

"A superb scheme, Tom, superb!" said Dr. Schein.

"Tremendous!" "Wild!" "Beautiful!" and other choice adjectives came from the others.

Mirrik snorted and bellowed in enthusiasm.

Jan beamed at me with pride.

Pilazinool stirred in his seat, twiddled with the fastenings of his left leg as though about to unscrew it, then changed his mind and waved a hand for attention. He spoke very slowly, telling us how impressed he was with my idea. In his judgment it was possible to locate the vault, and he thought there was even an excellent chance that it still would contain the robot.

"I recommend that we make contact with an observatory computer at once and learn if the location of the vault is indeed discoverable. If it is, I am of the opinion that we should discontinue work here and seek it out," Pilazinool said. "Aside from the globe, we have found nothing here that has not been found at all other High Ones sites. We are engaged in a routine and conventional dig. But I see the globe as the first link in a chain of evidence that may reach across the entire galaxy. The vault, perhaps, is the second link. Shall we remain here, drudging away at our little tasks, or shall we reach forth for knowledge elsewhere?"

Instantly we were split into factions again. The conservative people—Saul, Mirrik, Kelly—were in favor of staying here and exhausting the present site before doing anything else. The romantics—Jan, Leroy, Steen, and me—spoke for Pilazinool's point that we were better off chasing an exciting will-o-the-wisp across the galaxy than digging up another ten thousand inscription nodes here. 408b leaned to our viewpoint, not out of any romantic hunger for adventure but only because it wanted a close look at a High Ones robot. Dr. Schein seemed split between what he saw as our obligation to work the promising Higby V site down to the bottom, and our chance of finding something colossal on that asteroid. Dr. Horkkk, who had earlier advocated quitting here so we could concentrate on studying the globe, seemed now eager to keep on here out of pure contrariness, but I sensed that he too was at least partly fascinated by the possibility of tracing the asteroid vault.

We didn't try to reach a decision. Why draw conclusions until we know if we can find the asteroid? Tomorrow we'll call one of the big observatories and see.

But after the meeting broke up, we fissioned into several groups and went right on discussing. Jan and I were talking with Pilazinool, and the Shilamakka was not minded to sponge his syllables. In that smooth lathe-turned mechanical voice of his, Pilazinool said quietly, confidently, "We will find the asteroid, Tom. And the robot will still be there. And it will lead us to other and more astonishing things."

A Shilamakka doesn't use the future tense in quite that way unless he's delivering The Word. If Pilazinool is right, we won't be on Higby V much longer.

And Pilazinool specializes in being right.

eight

A very busy few weeks. We have all been working double and triple overtime, which is why I've made no entry in these memoirs for you, Lorie. Let's see if I can bring you up to date in one sizzling blaze of verbiage.

The important thing is that we are now committed, kneecaps, collarbones, and medulla, to my totally chimpo project for finding that asteroid vault.

It happened in easy stages, the way cataclysmic events often do. When you sink into quicksand, you don't get sucked—sploosh!—to the bottom of the swamp in one quick glunk. No, you're drawn in slowly thinking at first that the quicksand is just ordinary muck, that you can always pull out of it if you want to, that it's a cinch to get free in case you decide you didn't really want to cross that particular swamp. Suddenly the stuff is up around your shins and you get a little worried, and you move faster, thinking it'll do you some good, but it only mires you in deeper, but you remain cool and confident, and gradually, when you're hip deep and gently sinking, you begin to admit that your struggles are making things worse and that you're in the sticky for keepses.

Thus I found the globe. Thus we watched the fascinating scenes. Particularly the asteroid-and-rock-vault sequence. Whereupon I suggested finding the vault. Whereafter Pilazinool lent his vast prestige to the quest. Ipso facto we took the idea seriously and went so far as to obtain the computer simulations I talked about. And then—and then—

One of the first steps in our ensnarement involved borrowing a telepath from the military base, so we could transmit our astronomical data to the observatory. We did *not* request Marge Hotchkiss. I made it clear to Dr. Schein that her attitude wasn't a positive one. Dr. Schein spoke to the base commander and we got one of the other TPs stationed on Higby V. Perhaps you know him: Ron Santangelo.

In the flesh he's a pale young man, nineteen at most, with watery blue eyes, thin sandy hair, and a generally fragile look. He gives the appearance of being poetic. Maybe he is. He once had a Virangonian tattoo job on both cheeks, but evidently thought better of it and had it removed; not by a very capable surgeon, though, because the outline scars still show. I'll bet he hates it here.

His first job for us was to make TP contact with Luna City Observatory and find out if they could handle the work we needed. We chose Luna City after a long debate; half a dozen other observatories were proposed, including one on Thhh, the Marsport one, and even old Mount Palomar, but we decided to go to the biggest and best. It doesn't cost any more to call Luna than it does Marsport or Mount Palomar, after all, and the time factor would be the same. And despite Dr. Horkkk's chauvinism, neither Thhhian astronomers nor Thhhian computers are in neutrino-buzzing distance of those of Earth and Earth's colonies; everybody knows that.

Santangelo obligingly went through bimpty-bump relay posts and transmitted our message to Luna City, a task that took about an hour. The folks on the other end already knew about our globe, from the news release we had sent out, and naturally they were quite excited at taking part in the search for the High Ones' hidden asteroid.

I don't think they knew what they were letting themselves in for. Nor did we. Quicksand. Utter quicksand.

We had to get our data to the observatory, now. The easiest way to accomplish that would have been to ship our photos to Luna aboard the next ultraspace vessel to call at Higby V. One of the regular multihoppers was due here in the middle of September and would be reaching the Sol system in its roundabout way a couple of weeks after Christmas. Luna City could process the material, reply by TP, and give us our info by the end of January, say.

But that seemed like an impossibly long time from now. So the three bosses conferred and decided to send the data to Luna City via TP. That's right—TP transmission of photographs. I can feel you shuddering from here.

Ron Santangelo looked paler than ever when we told him what we wanted him to do. Give him credit, though: he didn't run off screaming into the night. Instead he served as our technical advisor. Here's how he had us handle the job.

We began by making a standard stereo photo of the thousand-parsec galactic scene that the robot sequence opens with. Jan did most of the darkroom work, and came forth with a fine blowup, two meters long, one meter high, and with an apparent perceptual depth of one meter. Then we rephotographed this, using a trick camera from the military base that is capable of stepping down a stereo hologram into an ordinary antiquated two-dimensional photo. What it gave us was a sheaf of prints, each representing a flat section of the stereo; it was as though we had taken a knife and sliced that three-dimensional print into a bunch of layers.

It took a little over a week to do all this, with an assist from Dr. Horkkk's little computer, which we had to reprogram completely in the process. (He is now restoring the original program for linguistic analysis, and doing a lot of cursing in Thhhian and many other tongues.) We now had our first astronomical shot converted into a form suitable for TP transmission.

Poor Ron.

He went off into a quiet corner of the lab to transmit. He labeled each photo, keying in its place in the overall picture so that the composite could be put back together again at the other end. Then he broke every photo into a series of ten-square-centimeter grids. And then he started transmitting the contents of each grid to other members of the TP relay network.

I hadn't ever given much thought to methods of transmitting pictures by TP. In my naive and ill-informed way, I assumed that Ron was somehow going to send *descriptions* of each section of the photo. (You know: "Up here, two point eight five centimeters from the top left-hand corner, we've got a star that covers point nine millimeters, and is sort of fuzzy on the right-hand side. . . .") But of course that would never have worked. At best it would have produced a vague approximation of the original photos; and computations based on vague approximations tend to come out as even vaguer approximations. As they say in the data-processing trade, garbage in, garbage out.

Jan had a much more imaginative idea of how Ron was going to do it. She said, "I think he'll stare at each little piece of the grid until he's got it firmly in his mind. Then he'll transmit the entire image to the next TP in the relay chain, and on and on so that the picture reaches Luna City in all its original detail."

Certainly that was superior to trying to break the image down into words and measurements and dictating those. But there was one little flaw in Jan's scheme, and Steen Steen found it.

"How," he/she asked nastily, "does the final TP in the chain convert the transmitted mental image back into a photograph?"

Jan thought there might be some kind of machine that the TP could think the image into, which would mechanically transform it into a photo. Saul Shahmoon overheard that and clapped his hands.. "A thought-activated camera! Wonderful! Wonderful! When shall it be invented?''

"There isn't any such thing?" Jan asked.

"Sadly, no," said Saul.

It turned out that Ron Santangelo transmitted the details of those photos in the most prosaic way possible, using a method that was invented more than three hundred years ago so that the primitive space satellites and flybys could relay photographs of the Moon and the planets to Earth. We were embarrassed for our ignorance when we found out about it. All that was done—as I suppose you know—was that each little photo was placed before an optical scanner that converted its gradations of black and white into data bits. Ron then took the printout and transmitted it to the TP network. He didn't send images, he didn't send verbal descriptions; he sent stuff that went like this:

```
0000000000000010000000000000
0000000000000110000000000000
0000000000000111000000000000
0000000000000111000000000000
0000000000000111000000000000
0000000000000111000000000000
0000000000000111000000000000
```

And so on and on and on, thousands of bits for each photo.

At the far end of the relay, a computer would with the greatest of ease turn the combinations of 1s and 0s back into shades of light and dark and produce photo-replications. *Then* something similar to Jan's suggestion would be used. Our TP would indeed transmit the whole image of the photo to a specially-trained TP at the Luna City Observatory, who would compare the image against the replication and carefully make any necessary corrections. Finally the whole giboo could be assembled into a duplicate of the original three-dimensional photo and handed over to the astronomers, who could at last begin their work.

What a cosmic headache!

More to the point: what a cosmic expense!

Ron looked a little grim as he began his task, but the rest of us, having no hint of the immensity of it, were in high spirits. We trotted to and fro between the scanner and Ron, bringing him his pages of gray printout with their interminable 1s and 0s, and he sat there, getting paler and thinner and more poetic-looking by the minute, boosting the data into the TP net. Meanwhile Jan and Saul were already at work making a two-dimensional breakdown of the second photo we planned to transmit, the close-up of the white dwarf and its stellar neighbors.

Ron didn't collapse until the third day.

We non-TPs talk a lot about the soaring wonder of roving the galaxy with your mind. What we overlook, I guess, is the terrible strain of it. And the fact that drudgery is drudgery, with or without TP.

Ron *gave*. He worked maximum hours, two hours on, two hours off, four shifts a day; and during the rest shifts he seemed impatient to get back to transmitting. God knows why. He had become as involved in the project as we were, but there couldn't have been much thrill for him in sitting in the corner going 0000011100000 for eight hours a day.

The strain showed on him. He sweated a lot, and his tattoo scars mysteriously became more visible, glowing against his sunken cheeks. Why a quiet, reserved lad like that had ever let a Virangonian needle artist go to work on him is beyond me. The tattoos were wildly obscene, too—according to the Virangonian notion of obscenity. That's what Mirrik said. Someday I'd like to know why Virangonians consider mouths obscene, because that's what Ron had on his cheeks: two big toothy tattooed mouths.

We could see him caving in hour by hour, and we tried to be good to him, to help him relax. Mirrik told stories, and Steen Steen did a pretty fair juggling act, and Jan took him for a walk and came back looking a little flushed and rumpled. I wasn't too happy about that, but I told myself it was All For The Cause. By the second day Ron's data-transmission speed was about two thirds what it had been at the start, and the next day it was even slower. And he was nowhere near the midpoint of the job. On his fourth shift of the third day he stopped suddenly, looked around the laboratory, blinked, and said, "What time is it? Does anyone know the time? My watch won't tell me. I've asked it, but it won't tell."

Then he stood up and, as though all his bones had suddenly been pulled from his body, crumpled and dropped.

The base medic said it was simply exhaustion, ordered Ron not to do any TP work for a week, and hauled him away for a few days of deepsleep recuperation. There were two other TPs available on Higby V: Marge Hotchkiss and a gloomy Israeli named Nachman Ben-Dov. Since the communications net had to stay open for messages around the clock, this presented certain problems of scheduling. With Ron temporarily out of the hookup, Hotchkiss and Ben-Dov were required to put in twelve Earthnorm hours each day simply handling routine switching and transmitting assignments. That was four hours a day more than the supposed maximum for TP work, and left neither of them any time at all for us. Since they had already been working overtime for the three days that Ron had been transmitting full-time from our lab, neither of them took kindly to an extension of their duties. Particularly dear Marge.

Dr. Schein pulled some strings and we managed to work out a deal. First, it was agreed that the TP staff on Higby III, where some patchy farming settlements have been founded lately, would intercept all incoming messages bound for Higby V. These would be relayed from III to V by ordinary radio transmission; we undertook to pay the extra cost of this. That took about half the burden off the local TP staff. The military people were willing—grudgingly—to defer most outgoing messages until Ron got better, which also helped. The two TPs would still have to be on call four hours a day apiece for normal duties. But that left each one of them four hours a day for us.

We didn't want any more collapses, though. We decided on a pattern whereby Ben-Dov would come out to the lab and transmit for us for two two-hour shifts, while Marge was sleeping. Then somebody would drive him back into town and get Marge, who'd come out and do two two-hour shifts while Ben-Dov was handling the ordinary stuff at the communications office. Then Ben-Dov would get some sleep and Marge would go back to put in her four hours of office work. That gave us the four daily shifts we had been getting out of Ron, and still left the two TPs time to handle their real work without burning out. Our transmission times were different now, though. Ron had preferred to do his transmitting in one sixteen-hour burst, two hours on and two hours off for the full four shifts, followed by eight hours of exhausted sleep. But Marge and Ben-Dov didn't work that way. They kept shifting their sleep periods around, now knocking out in the evening, now in the middle of the day; they might put in eight hours of TP (four work, four rest) after breakfast and then eight more (four work, four rest) after dinner, with a nap in between. With sleepdrugs it's no trick to arrange your slumber pattern to suit your whims, of course, and you know all about the odd living habits of the TP tribe. It made life weird for us, though, since somebody had to be around to assist the TP, bring snacks, correlate the computer printouts, and so forth. We tried to maintain a normal digging schedule at the site—yes, we're still digging through all this—and yet have somebody available to hold the TP's hand no matter what hour.

Pilazinool, who needs one hour of sleep out of every twenty-four, did much more than his share of this work. Too bad, for his gifts were needed elsewhere.

We did manage to get most of the data transmitted. Marge was no joy to have around the lab, and even less fun to drive back and forth from town—I made a point of avoiding that assignment—but I'll give her credit: she's got superb TP stamina. She'd come in, pick up the data sheets, start sending, and hum along on the dreary job faster than Ron ever did, and with less apparent effort. I suspect she could have volunteered for overtime work and not suffered for it. But of course the idea never entered her head.

Ben-Dov was an odd one: about fifty years old, graying, paunchy, always needing a shave, not at all displaying the conqueror-of-the-desert image that most Israelis try to project. Yet behind his sloppiness he was made of iron. We talked a little; he said that until the age of thirty he had never even been outside of Israel, though he moved around a lot inside the country; he grew up in Cairo, studied in Tel-Aviv and Damascus, and drifted around to Amman, Jerusalem, Haifa, Alexandria, Baghdad, and the other important Israeli cities. Then he got the urge to travel and signed up for TP duty at the Ben-Gurion Kibbutz on Mars. Like a lot of other TPs he's kept on wandering, getting farther and farther from Earth with each change of post, but always volunteering for bleak, desolate planets like Higby V.

Mirrik, who as I think I told you is a big one on religion, became greatly excited when he found out Ben-Dov was an Israeli. "Tell me about the ethical constructs of Judaism," the huge Dinamonian bellowed eagerly. "I myself am Paradoxian, but I have studied many of the creeds of Earth, and never before have I encountered an actual Jew. The teachings of Moses concerning—"

"I'm sorry," said Nachman Ben-Dov mildly. "I'm not Jewish."

"But Israel—am I wrong, is this not the Jewish nation of Earth?"

"There are many Jews in Israel," said Ben-Dov. "I am, however, of the Authentic Buddhist faith. Perhaps you know of my father, the leader of the Israeli Buddhist community: Mordecai Ben-Dov?"

Mirrik hadn't; but he already knew a good deal about Authentic Buddhism, and his tusks drooped in disappointment as his opportunity to find out the inside data on the Laws of Moses faded. That's the trouble with the spread·of global communications: tribal structures break down. You get Authentic Buddhists in Israel, and Mormons in Tibet, and Revised Methodist Baptists in the Congo, and such. I must admit that Ben-Dov's Buddhism startled me, though.

Jewish or not, he was a fine TP operator. He and Marge between them waded beautifully through the data sheets. At the end of his week of rest, Ron Santangelo returned to the job, now on a work-sharing basis with the other two, and the skull-to-skull transmission of our first photo was completed. Back from Luna City came an acknowledgment; they had decoded the transmission and were going to work on trying to locate the zone of space shown.

I tried to do something a little shady about this time.

I called Ben-Dov aside after he had finished his stint for the day and said, "In your data-boosting, have you had occasion to link minds with an Earthside relay girl named Lorie Rice?"

"No," he said. "We haven't relayed anything through Earth."

"Do you know her? She's my sister."

He thought a bit. "I don't think so. You know, space is very large, and there are so many members of the communications net—"

"Well, you *could* relay something through her, couldn't you? By way of giving the other relay people a rest. And maybe if you did, you could slip in an extra thought or two, just to tell her that Tom says hello, that he's doing fine and misses her a lot—"

The way Nachman Ben-Dov looked at me, you'd think I'd just suggested that Israel give Egypt, Syria, and Iraq back to the Arabs.

"Wholly impossible. The basic rule of the TP service: *no free riders.* Such a thing would violate my oath. It might also get me into serious trouble. There are supervisory monitors, you know."

I dropped the scheme fast. I can't crank about Ben-Dov's refusal; he was right and I was wrong. But it would have been nice to send a word to you. I try to pretend that these letters really are reaching you, but I know they aren't, because I'm looking at the whole stack of message cubes that I've dictated so far. You haven't heard from me or about me since June, and I wish I could afford to let you know what I've been doing.

Anyway, our TPs finished sending the data of the first photograph last Tuesday. They started in at once on transmitting the stellar close-up. They're still busy with that one.

We have, in the meantime, gone on excavating the site, but our finds are drearily ordinary. By normal, that is, pre-globe, standards, we'd have been delighted with the wealth of High Ones artifacts we've taken from the hill. But now all of us right up to the three top men are inflamed by the wild urge to make spectacular discoveries, instantly, instead of going through the potsherd-and-crumb tactics of standard archaeology. It's bad science, we know, but we're palpitating to buzz away to the robot in the vault, leaving the rest of this once-promising site to lesser drudges.

And as of yesterday we find that we're absolutely committed to making spectacular discoveries. Because yesterday was the last day of the month, and the TP network rendered its bill.

Nobody had said much about the *cost* of all this frenzied overtime. The big thing was to relay the data; sordid matters of stash could be discussed some other time. Well, some other time has arrived. I don't even know how big the bill actually was. But you can compute it for yourself: we've kept a whole TP staff sitting skull-to-skull on an Earth relay for eight transmission hours a day over something like fifteen days.

The chilly fact is that we've spent our whole second year's budget on two weeks of TP communications.

As the finances of archaeological expeditions go, this one has an awfully big thumb. I don't know the details, but we have grants from half a dozen universities, a couple of private foundations, and the governments of six worlds. The purpose of all this stash was to pay our transportation to and from Higby V, to provide (modest) salaries for expedition personnel, to cover our field expenses, and to underwrite the cost of publishing our results. The funds thus set aside were supposed to last us for two years in the field. Nothing was budgeted in for extraordinary TP bills.

We are in trouble now.

Late last night Dr. Schein came over to me and said, "Tom, are you sure you don't have latent TP?"

"Positive, sir."

"With a twin sister who's a communicator?"

"I've been tested up and down," I said. "There isn't an atom of TP ability in me. My sister's got the family monopoly."

"Too bad. If we had a TP of our own, and didn't have to pay the ruinous official rates—" He walked away, shaking his head. Half an hour later Dr. Horkkk also approached me and quizzed me about possible TP abilities. Try, he begged me. Try to make contact with a TP. I felt like telling him to try to fly. Trying isn't enough sometimes.

Besides, did they really think that a freelance TP would be able to bypass the utility laws and use the communications net without charge?

As of this morning, this is the position: we *have* to find that asteroid, because we simply don't have enough funds to work our full two years on Higby V. Having crashed our stash, we now must come through with phenomenal results in relatively little time. One bit of encouraging news did arrive last night from Luna City. They've run the computer simulation and have indeed located the piece of sky our photo shows. They've identified Rigel, Procyon, Aldebaran, Arcturus, and a number of other familiar stars.

This is not colossally useful to us. The photo shows a cube of space with a volume of thousands of light-years, and finding a single white dwarf (possibly burned out) and a single asteroid in all of that is an impossible task. But what Luna City has told us is that the robot-and-vault sequence took place in our galaxy, which is some comfort. If the closeup photo enables them to pinpoint the actual solar system involved, we can take it from there.

We *have* to.

nine

We leave here next week for a star called GGC 1145591. That's where our asteroid is. With some luck, that's where our High Ones robot is too.

GGC 1145591 doesn't have a name, just a catalog number. It's seventy-two light-years from Earth, and the star closest to it whose name you're likely to know is Aldebaran, which isn't really close at all. However, a billion years ago Aldebaran and GGC 1145591 were stellar neighbors, which is one of the ways Luna City was able to trace our star. It amazes me that the astronomers are able to figure out the positions of stars a billion years ago, when the only data they have to work with are the observations recorded over the last four or five hundred years. But they're quite confident that they have found the right star. It's as if they took a film of the present-day sky and ran it backward until it corresponded to the billion-year-old picture left us by the High Ones.

Luna City tells us that our globe sequence was filmed precisely 941,285,008 years ago. If you ask me, it takes a kind of cosmic slice to make dogmatic statements of that kind. But that's what their computer told them, and I guess it must be so. It gives us one more confirmation of our own dating of High Ones culture.

GGC 1145591 is not visible from Earth. Or from anywhere else. It was a white dwarf 941,285,008 years ago, but by now it's pretty well burned out and has become a black dwarf. No heat radiation to speak of, and therefore no luminosity; as stars go, it's invisible. It was discovered about forty years back by a scout ship of the Dark Star Survey Mission. Except for that bit of luck, no one could have traced it for us, since it can't be located by optical or radio or X-ray telescopy.

We ran our TP bill a little higher by notifying Galaxy Central of our plans. Dr. Schein felt honor bound to let it be known that he was giving up work at Higby V. Zit! What commotion! I drove Dr. Schein to town so he could place the call. I wasn't with him while he was giving the message to Nachman Ben-Dov for relay to Galaxy Central, but when he came out of the TP office his face was dark and tense.

"They blew up," he told me. "The TP says they were practically spouting gamma rays. How dare we pull out of Higby V? What kind of archaeologists are we? What sort of madness is this asteroid chase of ours?" Dr. Schein looked as angry as I've ever seen him. "The phrase Galaxy Central used was dereliction of duty. I think they also called us unprofessional. They can't comprehend why we don't want to dig our full two years here."

"You tell them about the TP charges?" I asked.

"I didn't get to that part," Dr. Schein sighed.

He fell into glowering silence as we began our drive back to camp. Halfway there I said, "What are we going to do now?"

"We'll go to GGC 1145591 and find that asteroid vault."

"Despite Galaxy Central?"

"Despite Galaxy Central," Dr. Schein said. "There's no turning back for us now."

He sounded grim.

Over the next couple of days Dr. Schein, Dr. Horkkk, and Pilazinool were locked in almost constant conferences, and Dr. Schein made several more trips to town to talk things over via TP with Galaxy Central. Almost no information on any of this filtered down to us underlings. Sometimes Dr. Schein let a few words slip to his chauffeur, sometimes not. Meanwhile we went on digging, dating, playing the globe, and otherwise carrying on business as usual. This was the mixture of fact and rumor that we put together:

· Pilazinool is overwhelmingly in favor of going to 1145591 no matter what the consequences.

· Dr. Horkkk has had second thoughts about his professional reputation and now would like to remain on Higby V for the duration of our grants.

· Dr. Schein is wavering between the two positions, but generally feels that we have already compromised ourselves beyond repair and might as well go through with the voyage.

Also:

· That all our grants are being cancelled and we are being ordered back to Galaxy Central for a roasting. (This has been denied by Dr. Schein.)

· That Galaxy Central insists that we go on digging here, but is sending a separate expedition to 1145591. (This is still circulating, unverified.)

· That we have been cut off from our financial support, but Dr. Schein is trying to raise private funds for an immediate expedition to 1145591. (Confirmed by Dr. Horkkk and denied by Dr. Schein on the same day. Who's lying?)

The only thing we know for sure, and we aren't very sure of it, is what I said at the beginning of this letter: we leave here next week for 1145591. An official order has been posted in the lab to that effect. We're supposed to stop excavations tomorrow, begin backfilling the site, and pack.

All is confusion.

.   .   .

A day later, and confusion has been replaced by catastrophe. At least for yours truly.

All three bosses went into town after breakfast and spent the whole morning in TP communication with Galaxy Central. The rest of us started, in a halfhearted and uncertain way, the shutting down of operations. Most of us expected to be told later in the day that we weren't going anywhere and better open up the excavation again, so we didn't put much effort into the shutdown.

A little past noon our leaders returned. For the first time since the beginning of the crisis they looked reasonably calm. Dr. Schein was actually smiling. As they got out of the runabout, Dr. Horkkk said, "Everything is settled. We have Galaxy Central's permission, and we are departing on schedule for GGC 1145591."

That was all. They disappeared into the lab. A little while later they summoned Saul Shahmoon and Leroy Chang to a conference. Secrecy prevailed.

At dinnertime this notice was posted in our quarters:

MEMBERS OF THE EXPEDITION:
Agreement has been reached with Galaxy Central for suspension of operations on Higby V and for immediate transfer of activities to the solar system of the black dwarf star GGC 1145591. An ultraspace cruiser making a regular run will pick us up here on October 21. The following members of the expedition will depart for GGC 1145591 at that time:

Dr. Schein
Pilazinool
408b
Professor Chang
Kelly Watchman
Mirrik
Jan Mortenson
Steen Steen

The following members of the expedition will remain on Higby V until October 27, at which time a second ultraspace cruiser will pick them up and convey them to Galaxy Central, where they are to deliver the globe and other artifacts, and report on our findings thus far:

Dr. Horkkk
Professor Shahmoon
Tom Rice

It is hoped that these individuals will be able to rejoin the expedition at a later date.

I read the notice six times, and still didn't believe it. How could they do this to me? Ship me back to Galaxy Central? Cut me out of the expedition at its most exciting point?

Is it fair? I'm the one who found the globe. I'm the one who thought up the way we could have the location of the asteroid traced. And now—packed off to Galaxy Central while the others go on into the unknown—

While *Jan* goes—

I staggered across to the other dorm and found her. "Have you seen the notice?" I asked, though I could tell without asking that she had.

She nodded. "Isn't it awful?"

"Jan, how could this be happening?"

"It's a dirty deal, that's what it is!"

"What is this business about sending the globe back to Galaxy Central? I thought we decided not to do that. And to make me go with it—instead—instead—"

Jan said, "I've asked Pilazinool about that. He says it's Galaxy Central's pound of flesh."

"I don't follow that."

"Galaxy Central is furious with us for walking off Higby V, after so much effort went into planning this expedition."

"I know, but—"

"The bosses had to calm them down somehow. There were all sorts of negotiations, Pilazinool said, and finally they mentioned the globe. Galaxy Central wants that globe. We agreed to ship it to them if they'd let us hunt for the asteroid."

"All right," I said, "so it's politics. I don't mind that.

But why me? I found the globe, didn't I? I've got a right to see that vault! I—I—"

"Calm down," Jan murmured. "It's no use shouting at me, chimpo! I'm on your side already. You've got to talk to Dr. Schein and show him how unfair this is. Maybe he didn't even stop to think about it—just picked you to go at random. Go to him now. We'll all back you up, Tom. We'll sign a petition or something." She gave me a little kiss on the cheek, nothing passionate, a we're-for-you kind of kiss. Then she turned me around and pointed me toward the lab.

I went numbly over there and peered in. Dr. Horkkk and 408b were conferring. Somehow I didn't feel like asking aliens for mercy, so I said, "Is Dr. Schein around?"

"Went back to town," Dr. Horkkk said sharply. "What is it?"

"Pilazinool, perhaps—?"

"Went with Dr. Schein." More sharply, this.

"Well," I said weakly, "I just wanted to ask a question. About the three people taking the globe back to Galaxy Central. If it's possible, Dr. Horkkk, I'd like to be excused from that assignment. That is, if I have to go to Galaxy Central it means I'll miss close to a year of the expedition, and—"

Dr. Horkkk brusquely waved a couple of arms at me. "Take it up with someone else," he snapped. "These procedural matters are not my concern."

Dismissed. Zog out, Rice, I've got no time for you.

Dr. Schein and Pilazinool didn't get back to camp until late tonight, about an hour ago as I dictate this. They went straight to the lab and they're still there. I don't know what this is all about, Lorie. But I don't mean to let them sposh me like this without a fight. I've *earned* a place on this expedition!

. . .

October 16

I waited up half the night for Dr. Schein to come to the dorm, but he didn't show, and finally I fell asleep. In the morning, as we got breakfast, I went over to him and said tentatively, "Dr. Schein, if I could trouble you about a certain aspect of the notice that was posted yesterday—"

"Later, Tom, later. I can't discuss little details now."

Brushed off again. Everybody too busy for poor Tom. Glumly I went out to the site and joined the others who were backfilling. Mirrik tried to console me with Paradoxian proverbs. "He who suffers scorn and rejection," said Mirrik, "learns to grasp the roots of the sea." And also, "The higher powers reward us most tenderly by their absence from our lives." Furthermore, "He alone finds grace from whom grace is withdrawn."

"Very comforting, Mirrik."

"Meditation and concentration bring understanding, my friend. Perhaps this grief is beneficial."

"I'm sure of that," I said.

Then Jan came up to me, close to the fusion point and emitting a high-frequency zing. "Do you know what I just found out?" she demanded.

"Sure," I said bitterly. "Inasmuch as I'm a TP, it's no effort at all for me to read your mind and—"

"Shut up, Tom. I just learned who it was that drew

up the list of who goes to 1145591 and who goes to Galaxy Central. It was Leroy Chang."

"Leroy Chang," I said. "That's odd. Why'd *he* do it?"

"Dr. Schein asked him to," said Jan. "The bosses were too busy. He typed up the memo and ran it off. But don't you see, Tom? Leroy Chang! *Leroy Chang!*"

"Leroy Chang," I said again. "Yes, I heard you."

"But you aren't thinking! The list says that you go to Galaxy Central, and I go to 1145591 . . . and that Professor Chang goes to 1145591 also! Leroy deliberately arranged it so—"

"I'm tuned in now, Jan. I read it all!"

"Isn't it absolutely the *dirtiest*?"

"Where's Leroy now?"

"Packing inscription nodes in the lab."

I sprinted toward the lab. Mirrik called after me, "The universe is a reversible phenomenon, Tom! Paradoxian proverb!"

"Thank you," I called back.

For many weeks now—since Leroy had gone groping for Jan—I've been making a point of avoiding the company of Professor Chang. Leroy hasn't been cultivating me any, either, with good reason. Lately he's been a kind of shadowy, skulking figure, sniffing around the outskirts of things and occasionally casting a longing look at Jan or Kelly. I've regarded him as more pathetic than hateful—nothing but a creepy vidj of the kind you see in the grimier feelie theaters of big cities. Now, though, I was ready to demolish him.

I looked into the lab and saw him in back, indeed packing inscription nodes. Dr. Schein was also in the lab, and Pilazinool, and I didn't want to make a scene in front of them. So I said quietly, "Professor Chang, can I have a word with you?"

"Will it wait?"

"I'm afraid not."

"All right, what is it?"

"There's something out back by the site that I'd like you to examine. We don't quite know what to make of it, and before we backfill there, we thought we'd have you look at it."

He fell for it.

We walked in silence toward the site. But we didn't enter it. I halted in front of a mound of excavation tailings that we hadn't backfilled yet. A drizzle began. I said, "Let's stop here, Leroy. Let's talk a little."

"I don't understand."

"You will. They tell me you drew up the list of names of those who'd escort the globe to Galaxy Central."

"Yes." Guardedly.

"How come?"

"At Dr. Schein's request. It was just a routine matter."

"You routinely separated me from the expedition," I said, "while managing to send yourself on the asteroid trip. And to send Jan too."

"The globe," Leroy said, "was your discovery, Tom. I simply felt that you'd want to accompany it and look after its safety personally."

That kind of reasoning didn't impress me. "How'd you like me to throw you into the excavation?" I asked.

Leroy backed away from me. "What kind of talk is that?"

"Archaic belligerent primitivistic talk. You feeby sposher, am I supposed to sit back and smile while you neatly put me on an orbit heading into the sun?"

"I don't understand."

"You said that once already. Let me give you an old Paradoxian proverb: *The universe is a reversible phenomenon.* You know what I want you to do?"

"I don't like the way you're talking to me, Tom."

"Zog, man. I want you to put yourself in that gang heading for Galaxy Central. In place of me."

"But—"

"I'm going to the asteroid. And you're going head first into the pit if you don't cooperate."

I took a step toward him. He made some little blenking noises and looked sick. I hate bullies and bullying, but at the moment I didn't feel apologetic, thinking of the way he had bothered Jan.

Chang said, "These threats of physical violence—"

"—will be carried out—"

"—are disgusting, Tom."

"Into the pit!" I yelled, and feinted at him. He squeaked in fear. I grabbed him by the shoulders, but I didn't throw him in; instead I leaned close to his ear and said, "What would Dr. Schein think of you, Leroy, if Jan complained to him that you tried to rape her?"

Leroy shivered. He sagged.

I doubt very much that a rape-attempt complaint filed weeks after the event, under circumstances like these, would make much steam in court. But guilty consciences blackmail easily. Leroy glared at me, blustered a little, muttered that I was persecuting and maligning him, and then folded completely. "What do you want me to do, exactly?"

I told him.

He did it.

This evening a revised list of assignments was posted. My name now is among those going to look for the asteroid. Professor Leroy Chang has replaced me in the group returning to Galaxy Central. I won't miss him. Neither will Jan.

.   .   .

October 17

To continue this marathon letter. Today's news is about how I just outswiftied myself. I couldn't help it, though.

You know how it is when you get so spun up over a marginal thing that you overlook something really important? Old Paradoxian proverb: He who loses track of main point will oversleep when millennium arrives. I was busy maneuvering myself out of the Galaxy Central deal and failing to see what I should have seen at once. What all of us should have seen.

I hunted up Dr. Schein during my morning break.

"Sir," I said, adopting my humble-apprentice tone of voice, "I've got a hypothetical question. What if we get to the asteroid and find the robot and it's still in working order, and all? How will we communicate with it? How will we tell it who we are and how much time has passed?"

"It won't be possible, Tom."

"But it *could* be possible! We have a credential. A letter of introduction. Only we've decided not to take it with us."

"You've lost me, Tom."

"I mean the globe, sir!"

Dr. Schein frowned. Pursed his lips. Considered. Brightened.

"Of course! Of course, the globe, the globe!"

And rushed off to confer with Dr. Horkkk and Pilazinool.

The conference lasted an hour. Then they summoned us all to the lab for a general meeting in the middle of the day. Dr. Horkkk presided. Dr. Schein, sitting to one side, gave me a warm, fond smile. I was teacher's pet again.

Dr. Horkkk interlaced his arms, opened and closed his three bulging eyes in rapid sequence, stuck a few long, many-jointed fingers into his eating mouth, and otherwise went through the patterns that are the Thhhian equivalents of preliminary throat-clearing. Then he said, in his fussy, explosive little voice, "I wish to propose a change of plan. It will require unanimous consent, since the consequences may be serious. As you know, we have agreed to Galaxy Central's request that the globe be shipped there at once for study and preservation. However, a suggestion was made today that we keep the globe with us as a means of communication should we find the High Ones' robot. It could serve, so to speak, as a letter of introduction, establishing our credentials as archaeologists of an era much later than its own."

I admired the deft adoption of my own terms.

"That is," Dr. Horkkk went on, "we could demonstrate to the robot that we had found the globe and followed it to the robot, and that a great length of time had passed since its arrival on the asteroid. I can visualize other ways in which communication will be possible using the globe as intermediary. However, if we take it with us, we will be in direct defiance of our understanding with Galaxy Central. Therefore—"

He called for a vote.

All in favor of telling Galaxy Central to go sposh itself? Eleven hands in the air.

Opposed? Zero.

Carried unanimously. Dr. Schein now said, "Of course, there's no reason now for any of us to go to Galaxy Central. The recent order is cancelled. We will travel as a unit to the asteroid."

Damn. I thought for a while that I was rid of Leroy Chang.

ten

November 16? 17? 18? 2375
Somewhere in Ultraspace

A month has passed, I know, since I last fingered a message cube. Something about voyages in ultraspace discourages my impulse to communicate. I'm not even sure what day it is. There's an Earthstyle calendar somewhere aboard, but I can't bother to look for it.

We closed up shop on Higby V right on schedule, leaving the site sealed so that the next archaeologists to work it—hopefully, a less flighty bunch than we turned out to be—will find it intact. The cruiser arrived and picked us up on the twenty-first. We did not inform Galaxy Central that we've taken the globe with us. That makes us renegades of sort, but it'll be months before the bureaucrats back home find that out, and by then, maybe, we'll have some gaudy new find to calm them. As Mirrik learned after his boozy prance through the lab, any sinner can find redemption if the yield of his sin is spectacular enough.

Our ship is a standard interstellar cruiser, making an upper quadrant run between Rigel and Aldebaran. The stop at GGC 1145591 is slightly out of the way, but not too much, and wasn't hard to arrange. All it took was stash. Old Earthside proverb: Stash buys. We will have a rented planetship at our disposal so that we can search the GGC 1145591 system for our asteroid. It's already on its way there from Aldebaran to await us. That took stash too. Dr. Schein overdrew our thumb account long ago, but he has a glib way with computers and is running on credit now; we'll manage so long as Galaxy Central doesn't find out. May the Almighty Proton protect us if we draw a blank on this expedition—if we have, to use the fine medieval expression, gone off to chase the wild duck.

Our quarters are comfortable, as before. Spacious cabins, good library, recreation facilities, decent food. The crewmen keep to themselves, we to ourselves. Time blurs strangely aboard an ultradrive trip, and I find myself doing without sleep for what may possibly be two or three days in a row, and then sleeping for days. Or so it seems.

Everybody is much keyed up, especially Drs. Schein and Horkkk. They walk around perpetually surprised that they ever found the slice to abandon Higby V for the present quest. Dr. Horkkk, you know, is hardly a charming romantic liberated adventurous type, and as near as I can read his expression, he seems to be saying, "How can this be *me*?" Dr. Schein looks equally baffled. Pilazinool, on the other hand, is quietly confident, rarely unlaces his limbs any more, seems to feel that we have been blessed by destiny. We'll see.

My chief social accomplishment on the trip so far

has been to push Jan back to her obsession with Saul
Shahmoon.

I'm not sure how I managed that. I thought Jan and
I were working on the same wavelength.

I don't mean that anything very passionate had happened between us, or that we were about to apply even
for temporary marriage status, or anything remotely
like that. Our contacts have been surprisingly chaste.
We've done a little quiet biologizing, yes, but nothing
has occurred between us that would have been amiss
even in a fairly puritanical era. Maybe I'm a spineless
feeb for having been so restrained. We *are* adults. It
says right here.

However, despite all this chastity, Jan and I did
seem to be blending into a sort of team, and I don't
think anyone really minded it, Leroy Chang excepted.
As the youngest and (let's face it) most attractive
Earthfolk in the group, Jan and I were drawing a kind
of paternal approval from the others. They beamed at
us a lot. I always feel put down when I'm beamed at,
don't you?

They don't beam at us lately, because Jan's been
spending her time with Saul again. When I see her I
get the freeze, right down to absolute zero.

I don't know what I did or said or didn't do or
didn't say that made her chill off on me. Maybe I
started to bore her. I can be so terribly clean-cut and
bright-eyed, sometimes—my worst fault, you'd agree.

Maybe she's suddenly developed a terrific interest
in philately.

Maybe she never was in tune with me at all, but just
was using me to heat up some jealousy in Saul.

Who knows? Not I. Not a clue.

It's been going on for ten, twelve days now. Not to sponge syllables about it, I'm upset. I don't have any right to feel possessive toward Jan, considering that all that went on with us was a kind of glorified hand-holding, more or less. But I don't enjoy seeing her disappear into Saul's cabin for two and three hours at a stretch. With the door locked, too.

Having an imagination can be an awful burden sometimes.

. . .

One marginal benefit of this leg of the trip is that I've had a chance to get to know Kelly Watchman better. As you know, androids don't turn me on a lot, and until a couple of weeks ago I hadn't said anything to Kelly, aside from shoptalk as we dug, but "Lousy weather, isn't it?" and "Please pass the tingle tablets" and "Do you have the time?" and like that.

In fact, I don't think I've ever really *talked* with an android before. I knew a few at college, but they stuck together and didn't go out of their way to solicit the company of flesh-and-blooders, and I never tried to impose myself on them. And of course Dad has some androids working for him in fairly high-level jobs, but it didn't occur to me to make friends with them, either. I've always been a bit edgy and withdrawn around minority people; it's the well-known guilt feelings of the overprivileged classes that hold me back.

The night I first talked with Kelly was before Jan and I had started to drift apart. The reason I wasn't with Jan that evening was that she'd been feeling headachy and cranky, and had gone off to use the ship's nothing chamber in the hopes that a few hours cut off from all sensory stimuli would help her relax. Nobody else much was around, either; Dr. Schein and Dr. Horkkk were writing reports, Pilazinool and Mirrik were battling to the death over the chessboard, 408b had locked itself up for meditation, and so on. I was wandering around the ship, feeling left out and adrift, when Kelly came up to me in the library cabin and said, "May I sit with you a while, Tom?"

"I'd love it, Kelly," I said grandly, hopping up to draw her a chair, making a big chivalrous gesture out of it—the overcompensation of guilt again.

We settled down facing each other across a glittering single-crystal table. I asked her if she'd like a drink and she said no—of course—but wouldn't mind if I had one. I said I'd pass also. These genteel maneuvers occupied a couple of minutes.

Then in a low voice she said, "That man has been following me around all evening. How can I make him go away?"

I looked toward the cabin door and glimpsed Leroy Chang skulking in the corridor. Leroy is the only true skulker I've ever known. He glared at me really furiously, as though telling me how loathsome I was to keep getting between him and the women he was chasing. Then he stalked away, no doubt hissing a little and wishing he had a mustache to twirl.

"The poor quonker," I said. "He's got a sex problem, I guess."

Kelly flashed a dazzling smile. "When will he learn that I have no interest in helping him solve it?"

I felt a pang of sympathy for skulking Leroy. The android sitting opposite me looked fantastically desirable. Kelly's sparkling auburn hair tumbled almost to her shoulders; it gleamed and glowed with the sheen that comes only out of android creation vats. Her deep green eyes seemed like precious jewels; her flawless skin was not the skin of mere mortals; and in her careless way she had donned a clinging sprayon wrap that amounted to not much more than a bit of fluff up here and a bit more down there. She was a vision of seductiveness—a cruel joke played by the lab technicians who had put her together out of amino acids and electricity, because they hadn't conditioned any sex into Kelly at all. I imagine she could have made Leroy Chang happy in a way, if she had wanted to, but she didn't want to, and didn't even want to want to, and couldn't begin to understand what Leroy was looking for. The sweaty urges of humanity are as alien to her as the hunger of a Shilamakka to convert himself into machinery is to us.

Still, she was beautiful. The radiant image of voluptuous ninteen-year-old womanhood, a kind of dream creature. All androids are attractive, in a kind of standardized stereotyped way, but whoever had written the program for Kelly must have been a poet of the vats. Sitting there making sophisticated-type chatter with her, I felt vaguely like the hero of one of those tridim movies, forever enmeshed in romantic talk with mysterious beauties aboard spaceliners bound for remote ports.

However, nobody had been kind enough to hand me a script. I had to make up the dialogue as I went along.

Kelly, now that I had rescued her from pestiferous Leroy, seemed willing to sit in the library and talk all night with me, but after the first ten minutes I found that I had exhausted my stock of light conversation. It isn't easy to find much to say when you're aboard an ultradrive cruiser, locked up in a sealed container where contact with the rest of the universe is impossible. You can't even discuss the weather. Once you've talked about your reactions to the twisty-twisty of entering ultraspace, you've run dry.

For the sake of that mental image I had of myself as the star of a cool tridim (Tom Rice, Intergalactic Secret Agent), I had to find *something* to say. And so my mouth kept moving while my brain stalled. What is the one topic you should not discuss with a minority person? Why, what it feels like to be a minority person, of course. One should not risk stomping on toes, rubbing salt in wounds, focussing curiosity on a subject of which the minority person is heartily sick, etcetera. Naturally.

In horror and dismay I listened to my mouth say to Kelly Watchman, "I've never really had much social contact with androids, you know."

She was adroit. "There aren't very many of us."

"No. That's just it. You've always seemed so *different* that I've felt uneasy about you. I mean androids in general, not you in particular. It's so hard for me to comprehend what it must be like to be android. To be just like a human being in every respect, and yet not to be . . ."

My voice trailed off stupidly.

"Not to be really human?" Kelly completed for me.

I was appalled. "Something like that."

"But I *am* human, Tom," she said mildly. "At least, in every legal sense. That's been through the courts and settled. Whether you're conceived in a womb or in a vat, you're human if you have the human chromosome pattern, and you aren't if you don't. I do and I am." She didn't sound defensive or belligerent about it. She was simply stating facts. Kelly can't ever get really emotional, no matter what her chromosomes are like.

I said, "Even so—I don't need to explain this to *you*, Kelly—most people have this thing about looking upon androids as—well, not quite real."

Kelly said serenely, "Perhaps it's simply envy. The fact that we don't age, that our predictable life-span is three times that of naturally conceived humans, must stir some hostility. I myself came from the vat in 2289, did you realize that?"

Nearly ninety. As I guessed.

"It's partly that," I conceded. "But there's more. It's that we created you. That makes you—this isn't how I feel, you understand, but I know plenty of people who do—that makes you somehow occupy a rung below us in the order of things."

"When a man and a woman create a child, do they therefore look upon it as something inferior to them?"

"Sometimes they do," I said. "But that's a side issue. Conceiving a child naturally is one thing. Making life in a laboratory vat is another. It's almost godlike."

"And so," Kelly said, "you godlike ones show your godlike natures by feeling superior to the artificial humans you create. Even though androids outlive you and outperform you in most ways."

"We feel superior to you and inferior at the same time, Kelly. And that's why most of us dislike and distrust you."

She pondered that. "How intricate you naturals can be! Why must you be so concerned about superiority and inferiority? Why not simply accept all distinctions and concentrate on matters of real importance?"

"Because," I said, "it's in the nature of human beings to boost their own heat by chilling on somebody else. In the old days the victims were Jews or Negroes or Chinese or Catholics or Protestants or anybody who happened to be a little different from the people around him. We don't discriminate that way any more, mainly because races and religions and customs on Earth have become so tangled and mixed up that you'd need a computer to tell you who to be prejudiced against. Now we have androids. It's the same thing all over. You androids live longer than we do, you have better-looking bodies, you have all sorts of superiorities, but *we made you,* and so even though we're jealous of you we can take some pleasure out of telling android jokes and keeping androids out of our fraternities and that sort of stuff. Part of the prejudice thing is that the victim has to be somebody weaker than you in numbers, but somebody you secretly admire or fear. So people used to think that Jews were smarter than ordinary people, or that Negroes were more graceful and agile than ordinary people, or that Chinese were able to work harder than ordinary people; and so Jews and Negroes and Chinese were envied and despised all at once. Until it got so that everybody had a little of everybody else's genes, and so you couldn't think that way any more."

"Perhaps," Kelly said, smiling coolly, "the solution to the android-discrimination problem would be to create some sickly, ugly androids!"

"They'd just be the exception that proves the rule, Kelly. The only real solution would be to make androids capable of reproduction, and then intermarrying all over the place. But they say that the development of the fertile android is at least five hundred years away."

"Two hundred," said Kelly quietly. "Or less. Android biologists are studying the problem. Now that we are emancipated, now that we no longer have to be the slaves and beasts of burden you created us to be, we have begun to examine some of our own needs."

I found those words mightily unsettling.

"Well, perhaps eventually we'll outgrow some of our sillier attitudes toward androids," I said halfheartedly.

Kelly laughed. "And when will that be? You spoke the truth: prejudice is part of your nature. You naturals are so foolish! You run all over the universe looking for people to despise. You sneer at the slow-wittedness of Calamorians, you make jokes about the size and smell of Dinamonians, you laugh at the habits of Shilamakka and Thhhians and every other alien race. You admire their unusual gifts and skills, but privately you look down on them because they have too many eyes or heads or arms. Am I right?"

I felt as if I had lost control of the conversation. I had simply wanted to know what it felt like to be android, to hold such a complex place in modern society —but here I was on the defensive, trying to account for the idiot prejudices that H. sapiens holds so dear.

What got me off the hook was the arrival of Jan. She drifted into the cabin wearing the pale, ghostly look that people sometimes get after a few hours in the nothing chamber; her eyes were dreamy, her facial muscles so relaxed that she looked like a sleepwalker. Lying in a warm bath of chemicals like that, with your ears plugged and eyes capped, will do that to you. Jan floated in like one of the headless wives of Henry VIII, looked at me, looked at Kelly, smiled strangely, said, "Excuse me," in a silvery, trilling voice, and floated out again. Weird.

Somehow that punctured the discussion of racial prejudice. We didn't start it again. Kelly began talking about inscription nodes instead, and after a while I said good night and went to sleep. Since then we've spent several evenings together, sitting up late and talking. I think Kelly is using me as a way of avoiding the sticky attentions of Leroy Chang, but I don't mind. With Jan so conspicuously ignoring me, it's pleasant to have Kelly to talk to. And rewarding to discover that an android can be a real person in so many ways. There's an underlying core of calmness in Kelly that nothing can penetrate, and which to me betrays her artificial origin; but above that she's got moods, strong feelings, a sense of fun, sophistication, and a lot more. She tends to be a little defensive about being an android, in an if-you-prick-us-do-we-not-bleed? kind of way, but that's not surprising. I won't pretend that I've shaken off my prejudices. I keep thinking that Kelly is very human, *but* . . . and it's that damned *but* that won't go away. Still, I'm making progress.

It scares me a little to think that in a couple of centuries there may be intermarriage between androids and humans, with children produced. I wonder why that thought frightens me so much. Because an injection of android blood into our genetic pool may change us, maybe? *Improve* us? The thought hits me where my prejudices live.

But I won't be there to see it happen. That's comforting. Or is it?

·   ·   ·

On that ambiguous note I stopped dictating, ten days ago. It is now close to the end of November, and I pick up this cube again just to add the P.S. that we will be reaching GGC 1145591 in five more days. I doubt that anything significant will happen between now and then, and so I'm going to seal the cube.

Status remains quo in all ways. Whenever I see Jan, she's with Saul and they're deep in a discussion of the self-cancelling French stamps of 2115, or whatever. Kelly suggests I take up coin collecting in self defense. The idea doesn't seem practical. What the zog, I suppose Saul is just the better man. I wish I knew why, though.

Away with such trivia. The dark star awaits us.

eleven

We are very much on our own here. And things are extremely strange. I never imagined, when I picked a sedate profession like archaeology, that it would bring me to anything like this.

We are in a solar system that knows no daylight. We seem bewitched, transformed into gnomes, condemned to scuttle through dark tunnels lit only by a faint purplish glow breaking through from somewhere far above. But there are no tunnels. We are at the surface of the world. This is the condition of life here: unending darkness.

Even on Pluto the sun brings a sort of light, but not here. The sun of this solar system is a dead star, or rather one that is so close to death that we can sense the intensity of its final struggles. Our mood is subdued. We say little to one another. The petty conflicts that sometimes used to break out among us no longer break out. This place casts a mysterious spell. I feel as if I'm caught inside a cage of dreams.

The ultradrive crew that brought us here lost no time in clearing out. The cruiser landed on the third planet of the system, which has no name. (We are trying to think of one.) The crewmen unloaded our gear. Then they took off, fast.

Our rented planetship was waiting for us. It's a little undersized, but it'll do: carrying capacity of twenty-five, passengers and crew. For purposes of calculations the eleven of us count as twenty, thanks to Mirrik's extra tonnage. The ship has a two-man crew. The captain is straight out of bad movies, a veteran-of-the-spaceways type with seamed space-tanned skin and faded blue eyes; he chews some mildly narcotic weed from a Deneb world and goes around spitting everywhere. The weed gives him the smell of a cloying perfume, which is a little at odds with his tough-guy image. His name is Nick Ludwig and he says he's been piloting rental ships for thirty years. He's ferried a lot of chartered cruises of millionaires around, but never archaeologists. The copilot is an android named Webber Fileclerk, with the usual glamor-plus appearance. An odd team.

The planetship is both our transport and our housing, for we have no facilities for blowing bubbleshacks. Whenever we go outside, we have to run through a complete airlock cycle, which is a sploshing pain, and we have to put on breathing-suits. There's no atmosphere on this world. More accurately, there is one, but it's frozen solid. The temperature here runs maybe five degrees above absolute, and *everything* freezes, hydrogen, oxygen, the whole periodic table. Our suits are insulated, of course, but it would be a quick death if a joint sprang.

Once upon a time this may have been a fairly decent Earthtype world. It's a little more massive than Earth, and the gravity is maybe 1.25, which is to say enough to slow you down but not anything really uncomfortable. The atmosphere that lies around here in icy heaps was evidently our friendly oxygen-nitrogen mix. A terraforming crew could probably turn this place into a zingo resort planet simply by juicing up the thermonuclear reactions of the local sun until things thawed out.

The local sun . . .

We are obsessed by that sun. I dream about it, and I'm not the only one who does. When we leave the ship, we lose track of our purpose and stare at it for long minutes.

We wear telescopic glasses for a good view. There isn't much to see with the naked eye. We're only 110 million kilometers away from it, a lot closer than Earth is to its sun, but this star is small. And dark. Its visible disk is about one tenth that of the sun seen from Earth. We have to hunt around in the sky to find it, feebly flickering against the backdrop of space.

GGC 1145591 probably has a million years of life left in it, but as stars go it's on its deathbed. A star takes a long time to die. As it burns up the hydrogen that is its fuel, it begins to contract, raising its density and turning the potential energy of gravitation into thermal energy. That's what happened here, so many billions of years ago that it zaps the mind to think about it. Long before even the High Ones evolved, this star collapsed in on itself and became a white dwarf, with a density of tons per cubic inch. And burned on and on, gradually cooling, growing dark.

Now, as a black dwarf, it appears through the telescope like a vast lava field. There's the gleam of molten metal, or so it seems, with islands of ash and slag drifting on it. The mean surface temperature of the star is about 980 degrees, so nobody's likely to land on it even now. The ash masses radiate at about 300 degrees, and it's much hotter inside, where the compressed nuclei still generate considerable kick. Even a dark star produces heat, but less and less of it all the time. A million years from now this black dwarf will be dead, just a big ball of ash drifting through space, cold, burned out. The last flicker of light will be gone from this solar system and the victory of night will be complete.

We do not plan to stay here any longer than we have to. As soon as we trace the asteroid on which the High Ones installed the rock vault, we'll head for it.

This planet orbits the edge of the asteroid belt. There are thousands of asteroids beyond here, and may take weeks to find the right one. We begin with a very small scrap of information: the globe sequence showing a spaceship of the High Ones landing on a broad plain. From this it has been possible to calculate the curvature of the asteroid's surface; given that, we can compute its approximate diameter. Luna City Observatory helped us with some of this. There's a big margin for error, since we're just guessing at the asteroid's density, but at least we can eliminate 90 percent of the asteroids in the belt because they lie outside our parameters of size.

Now we're making use of our planetship's scanning facilities. Captain Ludwig has his equipment set up to track the whole asteroid belt; as each asteroid within the right size range comes within reach, he has the ship's computer run an orbit for it. So far he's found a dozen asteroids that seem to fit the specs. We'll scan for another week; then we'll begin to check the asteroids out, one by one. Let's hope we don't find too many more.

.   .   .

I think I'm starting to understand the troubles I've been having with Jan.

Every three hours somebody has to go outside the ship to set off a flare a thousand meters away. This has something to do with the measurements Nick Ludwig is making—something about triangulation—and I don't pretend to understand it. We take turns doing it, and Dr. Schein insists that we do it in twos just to be safe. This morning, when flare time came around, Dr. Schein said, "Tom, you and Jan suit up and take the flare, yes?"

It was all right with me, and I started toward the rack where the breathing-suits were kept. But as soon as Dr. Schein had walked away, Jan gave me a poisonous look and whispered, "Are you sure you wouldn't rather go outside with *Kelly*?"

"Kelly's got other work to do this morning," I said, not getting the point at all.

That was this morning. Jan suited up after all, and accompanied me outside in icy silence, and we lit the flare and came back in. But now I'm finally seeing the picture.

Jan didn't start cooling on me until after the night when she walked into the cruiser's library and found me talking with Kelly. I think Jan believes I've been fissioning around with her, that I'm having an affair with her.

I swear I haven't given a cough in Kelly's direction, not once. Kelly and I have become good friends, but purely platonic. There can't be anything real between us— and Jan knows it. Kelly just isn't the sort of one-in-a-million android who'd go in for biologizing. Or is Jan jealous simply of the *time* I spend with Kelly? Sometimes I envy androids. This business of humanity having two different sexes makes for all kinds of headaches.

.   .   .

We now have located seventeen asteroids that are possible sites for the High Ones vault. Captain Ludwig thinks that he's just about checked out the entire belt, but for the sake of caution he wants to keep scanning for three more days, that is, through December 20. Then we'll set out to inspect them.

Our chances of actually finding a billion-year-old vault on an uncertainly located asteroid suddenly seem fantastically slim to me. The others probably feel the same way. But we don't voice our doubts. We try not even to think about them. At least, I try. I start not to understand how we ever committed ourselves to such a chimpo scheme. Walking away from the juiciest High Ones site ever found, defying Galaxy Central, running up huge outlays of stash to romp around from star to star—! Archaeologists are supposed to be stable people, patient drudges who stick to their proper work year after year. What are we doing here? How could we have let this happen? Why did we imagine we'd find anything?

Dark thoughts on a dark world of a dark star.

Dr. Schein must be thinking similar things. Certainly this quest is out of character for him. The strain shows in his face. We're a little worried about him. He lost his temper at Steen Steen yesterday and really cranked the Calamorian over, just because Steen accidentally turned on a data mixer, fed two streams of info into the computer, and sploshed a couple of hours' work. Dr. Schein got so angry we all were shocked, especially when he said right to Steen's face, "You wouldn't have been here at all if I had had my way! You were forced on me in the name of racial tolerance!"

Steen kept his/her temper pretty well. His/her tentacles did a little twining movement, and his/her sidemantles rippled in an ominous way. I expected a militant denunciation of Dr. Schein's bigotry to come tumbling out. But Steen had been discussing Christianity with Mirrik earlier in the day, and I guess he/she was in a Jesus mood, because what Steen said was, "I forgive you, Dr. Schein. You know not what you say."

A silly interlude all around. But it was disturbing to see our good and kind and rational Dr. Schein screeching that way. He must be worried. I am.

.   .   .

As you know I'm famous for my subtle approach. So after I had had a few days to think about Jan's remark about me and Kelly, I worked out a subtle way to take the matter up with her.

We went out to light flares again. The rotation schedule called for 408b to accompany me, but I arranged things with Pilazinool, and Jan was substituted. As we emerged from the airlock and stepped out onto the icy plateau I said, "What did you mean by that remark about me and Kelly?" Subtle.

Jan's helmet hid her expression. The voice that came over my breathing-suit radio was carefully neutral. "What remark?"

"Last week. When you asked if I'd rather come out here with Kelly."

"I understand you prefer her company to mine."

"That's not so! Jan, I swear to you—"

"Hand me the flare."

"Zog, Jan, you're absolutely imagining things! Kelly is an *android,* for zog's sake! How can you imagine that there's even the slightest—"

"Will you push the ignition plunger or should I?"

I lit the flare. "Give me an answer, Jan. What makes you think that I and Kelly—that Kelly and I—"

"I really don't care to discuss it."

She walked away, turned her back on me, and peered up at the dark star in an elaborate display of fascination with astronomy.

"Jan?"

"I'm examining solar phenomena."

"You're ignoring me."

"And you're boring me."

"Jan, I'm trying to tell you that you've got absolutely no right to be jealous. *I'm* the one who ought to be jealous. Watching you lock yourself up in Saul Shahmoon's cabin for hours at a time. If you're in love with Saul, say so, and I'll zap out. But if you've been doing all this just as some way of paying me back for my imaginary affair with Kelly, then—"

"I don't wish to discuss any of this," she said.

Females can be pretty wearying—yourself excepted, of course, Lorie. What I particularly loathe is when they begin coming on with secondhand dramatics, handing out a replay of the big love scene from the last tridim they saw. Jan wasn't speaking out her feelings to me; she was playing a part. The Cold, Aloof Heroine.

Fight fire with fire. Old Earthside proverb. I could play a part too: Dashing, Impulsive Hero. Rush up to stubborn girl, whirl her into your arms, burn away her irrational stubborn frostiness with a passionate embrace. I did. And, of course, smacked the front of my helmet against the front of hers.

We stared at each other across the ten-centimeter gap that the helmets imposed. She looked surprised, and then amused. She wiggled her head from side to side. I wiggled mine. Old Eskimo custom of affection: rubbing noses. She stepped back, scooped up ice, smeared it over the front of my helmet. I made a snowball and tossed it at her. She caught it and tossed it back.

For about ten minutes we capered around on the ice. In our big, rigid breathing-suits we were none too graceful; it was like a *pas de deux* for Dinamonians.

Finally we sprawled out together, exhausted, laughing wildly.

"Chimpo," she said.

"Zooby quonker!"

"Feeb!"

"You too. To the tenth power."

"What *was* between you and Kelly?"

"Talk. Just talk. Nobody else was around that night and Leroy Chang was pursuing her, and she wanted protection. She's quite an interesting vidj. But she does nothing at all for me *that* way."

"Swear?"

"Swear. Now, about you and Saul—"

"Oh, that's old stuff," Jan said. "Absolutely pre-historic."

"Sure. That's why you've been practically living with him for the past two weeks."

"I've learned a great deal about philately," Jan said primly.

"Of course," I said. "He can't find anything better to do with a beautiful girl in a locked cabin than show her his set of Marsport imperforates."

"That's right. That's exactly how it is."

"I bet."

"I mean it, Tom! Saul has never *touched* me. He's terrified of girls. I gave him all sorts of opportunities, hints . . . *nothing*. Strictly from zero."

"Then why'd you chase him so furiously?" I asked. "As a challenge?"

"At first it was because he seemed interesting. An older man, you know, dark, handsome, romantic-looking. That was before I paid any attention to you. I guess it was a sort of crush I had on him."

"But he wasn't crushing back."

"Whenever I started getting the least bit biological he'd hide behind a stamp album."

"Poor Saul," I said.

"Finally I saw that it was hopeless. And then I started going with you."

"Except you went back to Saul after we left Higby V."

"That was only to make you jealous," Jan said. "To get even with you for fissioning around with Kelly."

"But I *wasn't*—"

"It didn't look that way."

"Evil's in the eye of the beholder. Old—"

"—Paradoxian proverb. I know," she said. "Well, you could have explained a lot earlier that there was nothing going on between you and Kelly, and saved me two weeks of stamp albums."

"But I didn't know that that was what you had against me. Why didn't you tell me?"

"And look like a jealous little minx?"

"But—"

"But—"

"If you had only said—"

"If you had only said—"

"Gabbling blenker!"

"Spinless feeb!"

"!"

"!!"

We broke up in laughter. I threw some more snow at her. She threw some more at me. We raced toward the ship. The hatch of the airlock closed behind us and we got our helmets off fast. . . .

Why do women have to be like that, Lorie?

Why can't they come right out and say what's bothering them? If Jan hadn't imagined all sorts of dire stuff going on between Kelly and me, and hadn't staged this deal with Saul to get even with me for my imaginary sins, we wouldn't have wasted all this time and given each other two dreary weeks.

Sometimes I think the Calamorians have the right idea. Putting both sexes in one body with a single brain eliminates these messy communications problems. If Steen Steen ever gets into a lovers' spat with him/herself, he/she has nobody to blame for the mixup but him/herself. I mean—oh, blot it. You know.

.   .   .

December 20

We have twenty-one asteroids on our list now. We blast off after lunch to begin searching them for the robot vault.

twelve

Merry Christmas
In the Asteroid Belt

Once you've seen one asteroid belt, you've seen them all. The one we're in doesn't differ much from that of our home system: thousands of planet-fragments moving in a maze of orbits. Most of them are irregular chunks of rock a few kilometers in diameter, or less. (We saw one of those that looked exactly like a broken-off mountaintop. Perhaps it was.) But the ones we're exploring for the vault are much larger than that, good-sized little worlds with diameters of 100 to 180 kilometers. Gravitational stresses operating on an asteroid of such a size wear down any projecting corners and force the asteroid to assume the normal spherical shape of a heavenly body.

We've toured eight of our twenty-one asteroids so far. No luck.

We use a two-stage scouting technique. First we put our ship in orbit around the asteroid we're checking;

as we swing around it, we bounce a sonar probe off it to locate large cavities close to the surface. Our instruments are sensitive enough so that a cave the size of the High Ones vault would show up. If anything registers, two of us then go down in landing pods for a closer look.

Most of these asteroids, being pieces of a shattered world, are solid throughout—no underground cavities of the proper size or position. (The High Ones built their vault in the side of a hill, remember. Since there's no erosion on a planet or asteroid that lacks an atmosphere, and no internal volcanic action on a place this small, that hill ought still to look the way it did a billion years ago.)

We've made three landing-pod drops so far, a false alarm each time. The very first asteroid we checked seemed to have a cave in just the right position, which we thought was too good to be true. It was. Pilazinool and Kelly made the drop, and when Kelly cored into the hillside she found that there wasn't any cave, just a big salt deposit within the hill; we had misinterpreted our sonar data. Three asteroids later, Saul and Steen made the drop, but discovered that the cave was a natural one. And on the seventh asteroid Leroy Chang and Dr. Schein went down, only to find that we had misread our probe again; what we thought was a hole in the ground turned out to be a huge pool of mercury, no less.

That wasn't a bad misreading. Captain Ludwig immediately hopped into a pod and went down to inspect.

"You've got a million credits' worth of quicksilver

out there," he reported. "Never saw the stuff frozen solid before, but there it is. You be smart, slap a mining claim on it fast."

We didn't know much about mining claims, but Ludwig did, and we gleefully let him show us the procedure. Stash is stash, after all. We radioed our claim to the nearest galactic message depot, 2.8 light-years away, setting forth the coordinates of this asteroid and filing notice of discovery of the mine. It will, naturally, take close to three years for our message to reach the depot and be recorded, but at least we have established incontrovertible proof of our filing the claim on December 22, 2375. Meanwhile, as soon as we leave here and come to a planet that has a TP communications office, we'll notify Galaxy Central by TP of the discovery, and make the claim official. It may be six months or even more before we have a chance to do that; but in the unlikely event that somebody else comes here between now and then, finds the mine, and hustles off instantly to file a claim by TP, we'll merely have to wait until our radio message comes floating into the depot three years from now to demonstrate our prior discovery. There's no way to fake that kind of claim: it takes 2.8 years for a radio message to travel 2.8 light-years, and once our claim is in, no one can possibly jump it.

We're cutting Ludwig in for 10 percent of the profits, and his sidekick Webber Fileclerk for 5 percent. That'll make them both a lot richer than they ever would have become as charter pilots. The rest of the stash goes to us, not as individuals but as an expedition; it'll be used to pay off the monstrous deficit we've run up. Galaxy Central can no longer accuse us of fraud, embezzlement, exceeding of budget, or other dire things.

We'd still like to find that High Ones vault, though.

·　　　　·　　　　·

December 27

Two days more have gone by. We've checked three additional asteroids, and we've found another possible site for the vault. Jan and I are going to make the drop in about half an hour.

Nick Ludwig is programming the entry orbits for the landing pods. Webber Fileclerk is fueling them. The rest of us are sitting around nervously, wondering —for the fourth time—if this is *it*. Another ten minutes and Jan and I will be getting into our breathing-suits. Twenty minutes and we climb into the landing pods. Thirty minutes and down we go. I've got that sense of an overture playing again—the curtain about to rise—

·　　　　·　　　　·

By zog, we found it!

No, that's no way to tell it, not with wild whoops and jubilations. Let me be more matter-of-fact, more mature. Let me tell it calmly, step by step, from the moment we got into our landing pods.

Landing pods—

A landing pod is essentially a miniature spaceship, designed for work in a low-gravity region, such as an asteroid belt. It's a cigar-shaped tube about five meters long and two meters wide at its widest point; thus it can hold only one passenger, who must remain standing throughout the voyage. Mirrik is disqualified from using the pods because of his bulk; Dr. Horkkk is too short, unable to reach some of the controls, and 408b is the wrong shape, being wider than it is tall, to fit inside. That leaves eight of us able to go down to explore the asteroids in pods; and it's just the luck of the draw that Jan and I were the fourth team to go.

We use landing pods instead of going down with the whole ship because it saves fuel. A landing pod has practically no mass, and these asteroids have practically no gravitational pull, and so it takes only the slightest kick to reach escape velocity. Why bother maneuvering a bulky ship into a landing orbit when a couple of explorers in pods can whisk down, look around, and whisk up again? Especially when we're not sure we'll find what we're looking for.

Jan and I climbed into our breathing-suits and clumped ponderously down the corridor to the pod room. The pods were ready in the ejection chutes, lying down with their upper halves unhinged and pulled back. I got into my pod, Jan into hers, and Pilazinool and Steen swung the lids down on us. Miscellaneous clanking sounds told me that the pods were being sealed. A couple of thousand years ticked by. I used up some of the time by studying the control panel mounted just in front of my face. The round green knob would open the pod. The square red knob next to it would close it. The triangular black knob would bolt it. The long yellow lever to my right was a manual blast starter. The long white lever to my left was a steering rod.

They say that running a landing pod on manual is no harder than driving a car on manual. Maybe so. But the last time I drove a car on manual was when I qualified for my license, and I didn't care much for the sensation; it spins me to think of whole nations of drivers, a couple of centuries ago, at loose on the road and supposed to drive their cars *themselves*, instead of letting the traffic-control computers do the job. And as I got into the landing pod I wasn't too eager to have to pilot it back from the asteroid myself, either. Of course, I didn't expect to have to. Ludwig runs the pods by remote from the ship. But if the telemetry line failed, somehow—

Anyway, they shot us down the chute and into space.

Jan's pod went first. I followed her out of the ejector tube twenty seconds later. As I cleared the ship I felt a faint vibration near my shoulder blades: the ship computer was firing my nitrogen jets to insert the pod into the entry orbit Ludwig had programmed. I went hurtling feet-first toward the asteroid.

By leaning forward in the pod and peering down my nose and through my pod's viewscreen, I caught a glimpse of the silvery tube that contained Jan, zipping along below me. Her velocity and mine were identical, so that we seemed held together by a chain; but the asteroid appeared to be coming up at us at a fantastic speed. Something's wrong, I told myself. We're traveling too fast. We're going to smash into that asteroid like a couple of meteors. We'll split the asteroid in half.

Right on schedule, my tail-jets started firing. The pod decelerated and floated neatly down to its planned impact point on the asteroid.

Landing was a gentle bump. Instantly the four landing-jacks sprang forth to anchor the pod. I waited about ten seconds to be certain the pod was stable; then I twisted hard on the round green knob. The pod popped open.

I stood in the middle of a grim, terrible landscape. No breeze had ever blown here; no drop of rain had ever fallen; no living thing, not even a microbe, had called this place home. To my left, the plain on which I had landed curved away swiftly to the foreshortened horizon; to my right and straight ahead there ran a range of hills that looked like shrunken mountains, sawtoothed and jagged. The surface of the land was bare: no plants, no soil, no ice, only raw rock, pock-marked by the meteor collisions of billions of years. I remember the first time I visited Luna, Lorie; I was twelve years old and had never imagined that any place could look so desolate. But Luna is a lovely garden, compared with this asteroid.

As I glanced around, I felt suddenly sure: *this is the place!* In my mind I played for the millionth time the sequence of the globe, saw the plain on which the ship of the High Ones had come down, saw the low hills, the craters, everything. Everything matched. The only thing missing was the pink glow on the flanks of the hills, the pale light of the white-dwarf sun. That sun, much closer to death now, gave forth only a trickle of purple illumination; it didn't help me much, nor did the cold glitter of the stars. I switched on my helmet lamp.

Jan's pod had come down about a thousand meters

away, much closer to the hills. She was out of it and waiting for me. I waved; she waved back; and I started toward her. My first quick bound covered twenty meters.

Nick Ludwig's voice said in my suit speakers, "Remember the grav!"

So he was monitoring me. I looked up and saluted. But I walked more carefully. With gravity so low on this asteroid, a really good leap might be enough to send me a few thousand meters out into space. In a stately way I caught up with Jan, and we touched helmets by way of greeting.

Then we went together toward the hills.

She was carrying the portable sonar; I had the neutrino magnetometer. We halted in a cup-shaped depression in the plain, close to the hills, and set up our equipment. Turning on the sonar, we swung it slowly in an arc across the horizon, bouncing sound waves off the hills until the scope told us of the hollow place we were looking for. We carefully recorded the position.

We moved closer to the hollow place. I'll spare you all the thundering heartbeats and tense exchanges of knowing glances; let's just say that Jan and I were edgy and excited as we switched the neutrino magnetometer on and began to scan the face of the hill. As I brought the scanning beam over the area of hollowness, the needle shot way up into the blue end of the spectrum. Metal!

"This is it," I radioed calmly up to the ship. "We've got the vault right here!"

"How do you know?" Dr. Schein asked.

"I'm getting two different densities for this patch of the hill," I said. "They must have camouflaged the vault door with laminated rock. I pick up about a one-meter thickness of rock, with a huge slab of metal just behind it."

"And what's behind the door?"

"Just a minute," I said, adjusting the field of the scanner. Now the neutrino beam penetrated more deeply into the vault. The needle stayed on the blue; and as I moved the beam, the printout supplied me with a picture, in shadow-images, of the contents of the vault. It showed me the rear walls—dark, full of alien machinery—and the side walls, following the six-sided pattern of the globe sequence; and it revealed a dark, massive metal object sitting in the middle of the floor.

The robot.

"My flesh began to crawl with amazement," it always says in the old horror stories. Until that moment I was never able to understand how flesh could crawl, but now I knew, for my flesh was crawling in all directions. I had seen a billion-year-old film show me the construction of this vault; and I had seen the robot of the High Ones take up its position on the floor, a billion years ago, when trilobites and jellyfish ruled Earth; and here I stood, pumping a neutrino beam into that vault and seeing the robot still occupying the same place, and I tell you, Lorie, I was awed right out of my snuff.

I described the scanner readings to those in the ship. My suit radio dimly brought me sounds of shouts and celebrations from up there.

"Don't go anywhere," Dr. Schein said. "We're coming down!"

The ship shortly broke out of its parking orbit and went into an entry approach. Ludwig made a picture landing. The ship floated nicely down and settled smoothly in the nearby plain. Then the hatches opened and people came pouring out, and we held another festival of foolishness, dancing madly around the neutrino magnetometer.

Now all we have to do is get the vault open. That's all.

.   .   .

December 30

We're still trying, as I dictate this three days later.

Removing the laminated slabs of stone covering the door was easy. Kelly cored through until she touched metal, and Mirrik tusked the debris away. It took the two of them almost six hours to lay bare the entire door, which is about seven meters high, four meters wide, and, according to our scans, a meter thick. The High Ones didn't bother with a keyhole; and in any case we don't have the key.

We don't dare blast the door, not with all that High Ones machinery inside. And we aren't carrying a laser powerful enough to slice through a one-meter thickness of metal. We do have a power winch aboard the ship, and we tried it this morning; we fastened magnetic grapples to the door, ran cables to the winch, and pulled, but the door didn't budge and there was real danger that our cables would snap under the strain.

408b spent some time studying the hinge this afternoon. He thinks our best bet is to attack the door from that side: pull out the pin of the hinge, somehow, and swing the door open. But the hinge is about five meters long and the pin alone looks like it weighs a couple of tons. Furthermore, that thing hasn't budged in a billion years, and even on an asteroid without atmosphere or water there's bound to have been some degeneration of the metal, maybe even complete bonding of pin to hinge. In that case we're in trouble. We'll see in the morning.

.   .   .

December 31

A strange, grim, and busy day.

Unless we've lost track entirely, which is quite possible, this is the last day of 2375. But a New Year's Eve celebration seems irrelevant tonight, after the day's hectic events.

We went to work on the hinge first thing in the morning. Before making any attempt to remove it, we did a complete survey of it, with a tridim scan, measurements, holograms, the works, just as though it were a house beam or something that had to be destroyed in the course of an excavation. Not that the science of paleotechnology had much to learn from it, for it wasn't a particularly alien kind of hinge; there is evidently only one efficient way to design a hinge for a door, and the High Ones had hit on the same scheme used on Earth and everywhere else, so that the main point of interest about this hinge was how *un*interesting it was.

After this we got the most potent laser in the ship and started cutting. It took a couple of hours to slice the hinge the long way. At last we peeled it open and slipped the pin. Next we got the magnetic grapples out, cabled them to the power winch, and started tugging.

The cables went taut, and we cleared back, not wanting to be close at hand if they snapped. But the cables held. So did the door. Captain Ludwig threw the throttle of the winch wide open, so that it was pulling with its full fifty-ton force, but the tug-of-war remained a standoff. "What happens," Steen Steen asked, "if the winch pulls the ship toward the door, instead of the door toward the ship?" And it was a sharp point, because the pull the winch was now exerting was nearly enough to handle the ship's own mass and send it toppling forward.

The door yielded first.

It opened on the hinge side by about a centimeter. Ludwig changed a setting on the winch. The door slid reluctantly forward another centimeter. Another. Another.

What scared Ludwig—and the rest of us—was what might happen if the door suddenly gave up altogether and came flying out of its socket. The winch, to take up the tension, might very well haul the door toward the ship so fast there'd be a collision, and the ship would be demolished. Ludwig hovered over the controls of that winch like a virtuoso playing a chromosonic organ in a galactic music competition.

Slowly he peeled the door open.

We realized now that a bolt ran from the door deep into the rock of the hillside. That bolt was *bending* as the winch pulled on the door from the hinge side. Suddenly the bolt slipped from the rock; instantly Ludwig fed slack to the cable and choked down the winch, and the vast door toppled out of its frame, tipped up on one side, and fell forward, opening the way into the vault.

408b was the first to reach the open vault. It scrambled up onto the fallen door and stood there a moment, peering in and waving its tentacles about in excitement. This was the climactic moment of 408b's career: the specialist in paleotechnology was staring into a room packed with High Ones machinery in perfect preservation. Just as Jan and I reached the door, 408b rushed ecstatically forward into the vault.

A blinding bolt of yellow light burst from the top of the open doorway. For an instant the entire opening was ablaze. Jan and I stumbled backward, covering our eyes; and when we took our hands away the brightness was gone. And so was 408b. Nothing remained of it but two charred tentacles just within the doorway.

I've never seen death—permanent death—before. I once saw a construction accident, and a couple of pedestrian fatalities, but each time, a freezer truck arrived within minutes, and the victim was hustled off to a resurrection lab for repairs. You don't think of something like that as death, merely an interruption. But 408b was *gone*. Beyond hope of resurrection; scattered atoms can't be brought together and given new life. All its skills, its fund of knowledge, its hope of future attainments . . . *gone*.

In a civilization where most deaths are so temporary, a real death is a terrifying, shattering thing to behold. The rest of us gathered in a dazed little group in front of the vault. Jan began to cry; I put my arms around her, then found I felt like crying too, but I didn't. Mirrik prayed, Pilazinool removed and replaced his right arm about twenty times in two minutes, Dr. Schein cursed quietly, Steen Steen had a fit of the shakes, and Leroy Chang turned away, sitting on the edge of the door in a limp heap. Dr. Horkkk was the only one who seemed in full control of himself. "Away from the opening!" he shouted, and as we backed away he picked up a pebble and tossed it in. The lightning flared again.

We weren't going to be able to get into the vault. That was quite clear.

The death of 408b left us too stunned to proceed immediately. We retreated to the ship, where at Dr. Schein's request Mirrik conducted a memorial service for the paleotechnologist. Not even Mirrik had any idea what sort of religion they have on Bellatrix XIV, so he delivered a Paradoxian service, short and somehow moving. I won't try to reproduce it here; I can only recall one piece of it, the most characteristically Paradoxian of all: "Thou endest our time to teach us that time is without an end. Thou shortenest our days so that our days may be made long. Thou makest us mortal so that eternity will be ours. Forgive us, O Father, as we forgive Thee. Amen."

An hour later we cautiously returned to the vault.

Naturally our mood was dark and bleak; yet we doubted that 408b would have wanted us to go into prolonged mourning on its account when there was important work to do. We had rigged floodlights on the plain to work by during the cutting of the hinge;

now we moved them closer, so they would illuminate the interior of the vault. Keeping a wary distance from the entrance, we looked in, and I shivered a little with the chilly shock of recognition as I saw before me precisely the scene depicted in the globe sequence.

A six-walled chamber. Alien, mysterious instruments mounted in back, screens and levers and nodes and panels. Seated in the center of everything, ponderous as a tribal idol, the giant robot whom the High Ones left to guard this cave ten million centuries ago.

Time had not been able to erode the mechanisms within this cave. The blaze of light that ended the life of 408b was ample proof of that.

Nor had time harmed the robot. Incredibly, it still functioned; the combination of High Ones engineering skill and a protective environment of vacuum had given it the ability to withstand all decay. As our lights flashed across its domed head, we saw its vision panel changing hues in response—the robot equivalent of blinking, I guess. Otherwise it gave no sign of awareness. We confronted it, standing in a row outside the vault and not daring to go near, for many minutes.

What now? We were stymied.

Then I remembered the globe and our plans for using it as a means of communication. I reminded Dr. Schein of this, and he sent me back to the ship to get it.

The globe was mounted on rollers now. I pushed it within twenty meters of the vault entrance.

"Switch it on," Dr. Schein ordered.

My hand found the stud. The sphere of greenish light took form around me, widening until its perimeter reached across the threshold of the vault. Images of the High Ones began to swim in the air. Their airy cities, their rooms, their highways, even the sequence of the construction of this very vault, came into view. The robot's vision panel flickered madly; its glow raced through the visible spectrum, descending from high purple to deep red, and tumbling into the infrared, where I saw nothing but felt the sudden hot glow emanating from the vault.

The robot stirred.

Slowly, awkwardly, like an Egyptian mummy awakening from a sleep of millennia, the seated robot rose, pitching forward into a kind of squatting posture, then unfolding its pillar-like legs. We watched, frozen, terrified, fascinated, as the huge thing came to its full height of at least three and a half meters. It stood erect for perhaps a minute, testing its four arms, extending them as if stretching. It contemplated the scenes that were coming from the globe.

Then it began solemnly to stride out of the vault toward us.

Everyone about me panicked and began to run. I held my ground, more out of bewilderment than courage. And so I stood alone as the robot emerged from the vault and drew near me, a gleaming metal colossus nearly twice my own height.

Two of its arms reached down. Webbed metal fingers slid from recesses in the fist-like swellings at the end of each arm. Gently the fingers engulfed the globe. The robot took it and raised it high above its head, as though about to hurl it down at me with terrible force.

I turned and raced toward the ship, not bothering at

all to compensate for the gravity, simply leaping and bounding along. Eager hands reached for me and pulled me in.

I looked back. The robot had not budged. Like a titan holding a world in its grip, it still held the globe aloft. Motionless, lost in a billion-year-old dream, it stared up at it.

Two hours have passed now, since I came into the ship. In that time the robot has remained quite still; and we have huddled within the ship, baffled, frightened, yet deeply curious. Dr. Horkkk, Dr. Schein, and Pilazinool are once more conferring, up front in the ship's control cabin. I have no idea what happens next. We've fulfilled our gaudiest dreams; we've come straight to the asteroid where the High Ones built their vault, have found the vault, have found the robot still in working order. It's all like the kind of dreams that addicts buy in sniffer palaces. But now reality has broken in on the dream. The robot waits for us out there. One of us already is dead. Do we dare meet the challenge? Or, having made the archaeological discovery of the epoch, will we go slinking away in quonking terror?

I don't know.

And the robot still waits, as it's waited for a billion years.

thirteen

January 2, 2376
The Asteroid

Yesterday morning Pilazinool called for volunteers to go out and attempt to communicate with the robot. Jan's hand was the first to rise; mine followed, and then most of the others, with the notable exceptions of Steen Steen and Leroy Chang. The group that finally went included Pilazinool, Dr. Horkkk, Mirrik, and me. Jan didn't like having to stay behind, but I was relieved that she wasn't picked.

We crossed the bare rocky plain in single file, Pilazinool leading, Mirrik in the rear. All of us except Dr. Horkkk were armed; I carried a positron gun that was probably capable of blowing the robot up, but I wasn't sharp on using it.

When we were within twenty meters of the robot we halted and fanned out widely. Dr. Horkkk stepped forward. In his left hands he carried a little blackboard;

in one of his right hands he held an inscription node. The robot took no notice of him. It still stood as though a statue, holding the globe aloft, though images no longer came from it.

Dr. Horkkk slowly waved the inscription node from side to side, trying to catch the robot's attention. That took courage. The robot might be easily annoyed. After a few minutes Dr. Horkkk began to copy the hieroglyphics from the inscription node onto his blackboard, keeping the blackboard turned so that the robot could see what was happening. The idea was to demonstrate to the robot that we are intelligent creatures, capable at least of copying High Ones writing even if unable to understand it.

"Suppose what he's copying is obscene?" Mirrik murmured. "Or unfriendly? What if it makes the robot angry?"

Dr. Horkkk went on sketching hieroglyphics.

Gradually the robot started to show interest in him.

It lowered the globe to chest-height. It stared down at the small Thhhian, and the colors of its vision panel darkened; pale greens and yellows gave way to rich maroon, shot through with crimson threads. The equivalent of a frown, maybe? The colors of deep concentration? Dr. Horkkk's inscription node suddenly went blank, and a new inscription appeared. Calmly Dr. Horkkk erased his blackboard and began to copy the current message. The robot seemed impressed. From somewhere within its cavernous chest there boomed sounds that our suit radios were able to pick up.

"Dihn ahm ruuu dihn korp!"

Who knows what it means? But we assume that it's in the language of the High Ones.

Dr. Horkkk took another calculated risk. He put down his blackboard, stepped forward three paces, and said in clear tones, *"Dihn ahm ruuu dihn korp!"*

It was an excellent imitation. But for all Dr. Horkkk knew, he was accepting a challenge to a duel, casting aspersions on the robot's ancestry, or agreeing that he deserved to be obliterated on the spot. However, the robot's reaction was mild. It flashed a stream of violet light along its vision panel, extended its leftmost arm in a kind of beckoning gesture, and said, *"Mirt ahm dihn ruuu korp."*

"Mirt ahm dihn ruuu korp," Dr. Horkkk repeated.

"Korp mirt hohm ahm dihn."

"Korp mirt hohm ahm dihn."

"Mirt ruuu chlook."

"Mirt ruuu chlook."

And so on for several minutes. After a while Dr. Horkkk ventured to mix up the now-familiar words, rearranging them into new patterns to give a pretense at conversation: *"Ruuu mirt dihn ahm"* and *"Korp ruuu chlook korp mirt,"* and so forth. This had the virtue of showing the robot that Dr. Horkkk was something other than some kind of recording machine, but it must have been puzzling to it to be getting these gibberish responses to its statements.

Then the robot turned on the globe. The scene that took form about us was the sequence of the construction of the vault, beginning as usual with the wide-angle view of the galaxy, then the close-up of the immediate stellar neighborhood. The robot pointed to the pattern of projected stars. Then it switched the globe off and pointed first to the very different pattern of stars in the present-day sky of the asteroid, then to the burned-out dwarf star.

That seemed intelligible enough. The robot was telling us that it realized, from the astronomical changes it observed, that a vast span of time must have elapsed since it had been sealed into the vault.

The robot now made some adjustment on the globe, and the scene of the High Ones' city appeared. For several minutes we watched once more the High Ones moving solemnly and gracefully through their wonderland of cables and dangling structures. The robot cut it off, pointed again to the stars, pointed to Dr. Horkkk, pointed to itself, pointed to Dr. Horkkk.

Abruptly the robot turned and strode into the vault. It did something at one of the instrument panels in the rear; then it beckoned unmistakably to us. We hesitated. The robot beckoned again.

"Possibly it turned off the lightning field," Pilazinool said.

"And possibly it didn't," said Dr. Horkkk. "This may be a trick designed to make us go to our deaths."

"If the robot wanted to kill us," I pointed out, "it wouldn't need to trick us. It's got weapon attachments in its arms."

"Certainly," said Pilazinool. "Tom's right!"

Still, none of us went into the vault. The robot made its beckoning gesture a third time.

Dr. Horkkk found another pebble and pitched it across the threshold of the vault. No blast of lightning. That was reassuring.

"Shall we risk it?" Pilazinool asked.

He started forward.

"Wait," I heard myself saying, as another fit of heroism rushed through my brain. "I'm less important than the rest of you. Let me go, and if I make it—"

Telling myself that at the worst it would be a quick, clean finish, I leaped up on the fallen door, stepped into the vault, and lived to tell the tale. Pilazinool followed me; then, somewhat more cautiously, Dr. Horkkk. Mirrik remained outside at Pilazinool's suggestion; in case this did turn out to be a trap, we needed a survivor to explain what had happened to the others.

Instinctively we stayed close to the entrance of the vault and made no sudden moves that might alarm our huge host. We still didn't know if the robot's intentions were friendly. Much as we wanted a close look at those complex, cluttered instrument panels on the rear walls of the vault, we didn't dare approach them, for that would have required us to get between the robot and its instruments. The robot might not have liked that.

It turned to the instruments itself and touched one of the controls. Instantly images burst forth: the same sort of screenless projection that came from our globe.

We watched a kind of travelog of the High Ones' supercivilization. The scenes were different from those out of the globe, but similar in feeling, showing us all the magnificence and splendor of these people. We saw shots of High Ones cities that completely eclipsed the earlier one—cities that seemed to occupy whole planets, with patterns of aerial cables shifting and crossing and interlocking and apparently slipping in and out of dimensions. We saw grandees of the High Ones moving in stately procession through lofty, glittering halls, each being surrounded by dozens of robot servants of all sizes, shapes, and functions, catering to the smallest whim. We looked through tunnels in which vast machines of unfathomable purpose throbbed and revolved. We watched starships in flight, saw High Ones explorers landing on scores of worlds, stepping forth confidently equipped for every sort of environmental condition from dismal airlessness to lush tropical greenery. We received a dazzling view of this most incredible of civilizations, this true master race of the universe's dawn. The globe had shown us only a fraction of it. Brilliant, vivid scenes poured from the vault wall for more than half an hour.

Temples and libraries, museums, computer halls, auditoriums—who knew the purposes to which those colossal structures had been put? When the High Ones gathered to watch a gyrating point of light, as we saw them do, what kind of beauty did they comprehend? How much information was stored in those glistening data banks, and information of what kind? The starships that moved so effortlessly, seemingly without expenditure of fuel—the elegance of the housefurnishings—the incomprehensible rituals—the dignity of the people as they went serenely through their day's activities—all of this conveyed to us a sense of a race so far beyond the attainments of our era that our pride in our own petty accomplishments seemed to be the silly posturing of monkeys.

And yet . . . they are gone from the universe, these

great beings, and we remain. And, little creatures that
we are, we still have managed to find our way through
the stars to this place and to set free the guardian of
this ancient vault. Surely that is no small achievement
for a species only a million years or so away from
apehood. Surely the High Ones, whose time of greatness had lasted a century to each of our minutes, would
agree that we have done well for ourselves thus far.

And there was irony in watching this humbling display of glittering greatness, and in knowing that the
makers of that greatness had vanished into extinction
hundreds of millions of years ago.

"*Ozymandias*," said Mirrik gently, looking at the
images from outside the cave.

Exactly so. Ozymandias. Shelley's poem. The "trav-
eler from an antique land" who finds "two vast and
trunkless legs of stone" in the desert, and beside them,
half sunk in sand, the shattered head of a statue, still
wearing its "sneer of cold command"—

> And on the pedestal these words appear:
> "My name is Ozymandias, king of kings:
> Look on my works, ye Mighty, and despair!"
> Nothing beside remains. Round the decay
> Of that colossal wreck, boundless and bare
> The lone and level sands stretch far away.

Precisely so. Ozymandias. How could we tell this
robot that its fantastic creators no longer existed? That
a billion years of rock covered the ruins of their outposts on dozens of planets? That we had come seeking a
mystery locked in a past so distant we could barely
comprehend its remoteness? While this robot waited

here, the patient, timeless servant, ready to show its movies and impress the casual wayfarer with the might of its masters . . . never dreaming that it alone was left to tell the tale and that all its pride in that great civilization was a waste.

The projections ended. We blinked as our eyes adjusted to the sudden dimming of that brightness in the vault. The robot began to speak again, slowly, enunciating clearly, using the same sort of tone we would use in speaking to a foreigner or someone who is slightly deaf or a little dull in the skull. *"Dihn ruuu . . . mirt korp ahm . . . mirt chlook . . . ruuu ahm . . . hohm mirt korp zort . . ."* As before, Dr. Horkkk patched together some sentences in reply, with random combinations of dihns and ruuus and ahms. The robot listened to this in what struck me as an interested and approving way. Then it pointed several times to the inscription node Dr. Horkkk was carrying and spoke in an apparently urgent manner. Of course there was no hope of real communication. But at least the robot seems to think we're worth trying to reach. Coming from a machine of the High Ones, that's a compliment.

.   .   .

January 4

Dr. Horkkk has spent most of the last two days running tapes of his "conversation" with the robot through his linguistic computer, trying to wring some meaning out. Zero results. The robot spoke only about two dozen different words, arranging them in various ways, and that's not enough to allow the finding of a meaningful pattern.

The rest of us have constantly been going back and forth between the ship and the vault, taking full advantage of the robot's hospitality. By now it's quite clear that the robot isn't hostile. The death of 408b was a tragic mistake; the vault evidently was designed not to admit anything without the robot's permission, and if 408b hadn't impulsively rushed in the moment the door came loose, it wouldn't have been killed. Once we established that we were friendly organisms, the robot turned the lightning field off, and we now are welcome to enter the vault as often as we please.

We are getting bolder. The first day we stood around edgily as if expecting the robot to change its mind and zap us any minute, but now we've made ourselves at home to the extent of making a full tridim record of the machinery and taking plenty of shots of the robot itself. What we don't dare do is *touch* any of the machinery, since the robot is plainly the custodian of the vault and might very well destroy anyone who even seemed to threaten its contents. Besides, with 408b gone we have only the flimsiest notions of what that machinery is all about.

The robot has run its travelog several more times for us, and we've filmed it in its entirety. This is catching your archaeology on the hoof, all right: instead of digging up broken bits and rusty scraps of the High Ones' civilization, we have glossy tridims of the actual cities and people. Looking at them gives us an uncanny sensation. It's something like having a time machine. We've learned more than we ever dreamed was possible about the High Ones, thanks to the globe and what the robot has showed us. We know more about these

people of a billion years ago, suddenly, than archaeologists have ever managed to find out about the Egyptians or Sumerians or Etruscans of the very recent past.

The robot goes through the same curious pantomime routine whenever we visit it. It points to us,
points to itself, points to the stars. Over and over.
Pilazinool argues that the robot is telling us that it
would like to lead us somewhere—to some other vault,
maybe, or even to a planet once inhabited by the High
Ones. Dr. Horkkk, as usual, disagrees. "The robot is
merely discussing origins," Dr. Horkkk says. "It is indicating that both itself and ourselves come from
worlds outside the solar system of GGC 1145591.
Nothing more than that."

I like to think Pilazinool is right. But I don't know,
and I doubt that we'll ever know.

Communicating by pantomime isn't terribly satisfy-
ing.

.   .   .

Three hours have gone by since the foregoing, and
everything has turned upside down again. Now the
robot is talking to us. In Anglic.

Steen Steen and I were sent across to the vault to get
some stereo shots of one instrument panel, because we
had botched the calibration on the first try. We found
the robot busy in one corner with its back to us. Since
it was taking no notice of us, we quietly went about
our business.

Five minutes later the robot turned and came clanking over. It extended one arm and aimed an intricate

little gadget at us. I thought it was a gun and I was too scared to move.

The robot said, slowly, with great effort:

"Speak . . . words . . . to . . . this."

I did a quick spectrum trip of astonishment. So did Steen, whose mantle fluttered within his/her breathing-suit.

"It *was* speaking Anglic?" I said to Steen.

"It was. Yes."

The robot said again, more smoothly, "Speak words to this."

I took a close look at the gadget in its hand. It wasn't a gun. It consisted of an inscription node with a tesseract-shaped puzzle-box mounted at one end. Within the struts of the puzzle-box glowed a deep crimson radiance.

"Words of you," the robot said. "More. To this."

The situation began to acquire some spin for me. The robot had been listening to us speak—recording our words, prying into them for meanings—and had taught itself Anglic. And now it wanted to increase its vocabulary. Perhaps, I thought, an inscription node with a puzzle-box attached is a kind of recorder. (I was wrong about that.)

Steen figured this out a fraction of a second ahead of me. He/she nudged me aside, put the voice-output of his/her breathing-suit close to the glowing end of the puzzle-box, and began rapidly to speak—in Calamorian! He/she spewed forth at least a dozen sentences in his/her native tongue before I woke up, grabbed him/her, and pulled him/her away from the robot.

"Get your sploshing hands off me!" Steen shouted.

"You idiot, what was the idea of speaking Calamorian?"

"To program the robot's translating machine!" Indignantly. "Why can't it be given words of a civilized language?"

I was so furious over Steen's stupid militancy that I overlooked the important thing he/she had said, for a moment. I said, "You know damn well that Anglic is the official language of this expedition, and you've agreed to use it throughout. If we're going to give this robot words, they ought to be in only one language, and that language should be—"

"The robot should have a chance to know that Anglic is not the only language in the cosmos! This suppression of the Calamorian language is an act of racial genocide! It—"

"Shut up," I said, not very tolerant of Steen's outraged racial pride. Then I reacted to the right thing at last. "—*translating machine?*"

Of course.

Inscription nodes and puzzle-boxes weren't separate artifacts. They were meant to work together, as this robot had assembled them. And they weren't recording devices, either.

They were machines for converting the babble of primitive barbarian races into the language of the High Ones.

Steen had seen this quickly, and wanted to get his/her own wonderful Calamorian language into the record, in defiance of expedition agreements. Maybe doing it enhanced his sense of racial pride, but it also quonked up our chances of quick communication with the robot, since it had placed a dozen incompatible sentences on the record. No translating machine ever invented would get anywhere operating under the assumption that what Steen had just blurted and what the rest of us had been saying were both the same language.

I warned Steen not to try it again. Steen gave me a surly look; but he/she had scored the intended point and now subsided, leaving me a clear shot at the translating machine.

I bent close to it.

Then I wondered what I ought to say.

Words wouldn't come. Steen Steen had probably bellowed some glib testimonial to the everlasting merits of the Calamorian people, but I wasn't about to do that, and I developed a paralyzing case of mike fright as I tried to imagine the most useful and appropriate possible statements.

The robot said encouragingly, "Speak words of you to this."

I said, "What kind of words? Any words?"

Then silence. Steen laughed at me.

I said, "My name is Tom Rice. I was born on the planet Earth of the sun Sol. I am twenty-two years old."

I stopped again, as if the machine needed time to digest one set of statements before receiving another. It didn't, I now know.

"Speak more words," prompted the robot.

I said, "The language I am speaking is Anglic, which is the most important language of Earth. The language spoken by the last voice was Calamorian. This is a language of another world in a different solar system."

As I spoke, I saw streams of High Ones hieroglyphics rippling along the surface of the inscription node. The gadget was converting my sounds into the written characters of the ancient language. What good that did was hard to say, in terms of communication. When I write *Dihn ruuu mirt korp*, I'm converting the robot's sounds into our kind of alphabetic writing, but I'm not getting one step closer to understanding what those sounds mean.

It must have helped, though. Because the speaking vocabulary of the robot expanded from minute to minute.

"Say name of other one," it said.

"He/she is Steen Steen of Calamor. We have come here to seek information about the builders of this vault."

"Say more names of things."

I indicated and named the vault, the door, the ship, the heavens, and as much else as was within pointing range. Carefully choosing my words, I spelled out the fact that we knew that a great deal of time had passed since the construction of the vault. I tried to explain that we were archaeologists who had excavated many remains of the High Ones, but that no member of any existing species had ever encountered a living High One. And so on.

The robot studied the changing hieroglyphics on the inscription node with intense interest, but confined its statements to brief, brusque commands to go on talking. By now the translating machine had absorbed a healthy chunk of data. By now it had struck me that we ought to be letting the others in on what was going on, too, and I said to Steen, "Switch to ship frequency and call Dr. Horkkk here."

"While you feed the robot with poisonous lies?" Steen said. "*You* call!"

Resisting the impulse to kick Steen in the ribs, if Steen has ribs, I switched channels briefly, summoned everyone from the ship, and cut back to vocal output. The robot wanted more words . . . and more . . . and lots more. It soaked them up.

Dr. Horkkk and Pilazinool arrived, with the others not far behind. I explained the situation. Dr. Horkkk began to glow with excitement. "Keep talking," he said.

I kept talking.

I talked myself hoarse, and then Jan took over, and after her, Saul Shahmoon. It didn't matter much what we said; we were stocking a high-powered computer with data, in essence, and the computer would take care of sorting things out and making sense of them. Dr. Horkkk seemed to tingle in amazement and perhaps a sort of dismay, for such a sense-from-noise machine was exactly what he had been trying without success to develop in his whole career.

After more than an hour the robot was satisfied.

"No more words," it said. "The rest will fit in by themselves."

Translation: the machine now was sufficiently stocked with Anglic words. It would arrange them, make them accessible to the robot, and deal with additions to its vocabulary by interpreting them in context as they came along.

The robot was silent for perhaps five minutes, studying the ebb and flow of hieroglyphics on the inscription node. We didn't dare speak.

Then it said, in fluent Anglic that reproduced my own accent and pronunciation and even tone of voice, "I will name myself for you. I can be called Dihn Ruuu. I am a machine produced to serve the Mirt Korp Ahm, whom you call the High Ones. The meaning of my name is Machine To Serve. My purpose is to remain in readiness so that I may serve the Mirt Korp Ahm if they come back to this solar system."

Another long silence. Dihn Ruuu seemed to be waiting for questions.

Pilazinool said, "How long has it been since the Mirt Korp Ahm were on this place?"

"How shall I say the time?" the robot asked.

"That's a tough one," Pilazinool muttered. "We haven't defined our units."

Dr. Horkkk took over, and I must say he performed brilliantly. "Our basic unit is the second," he said. "The sound I will make is one second in length." He flashed an order back to the ship's computer, which obligingly generated a tone lasting one second. Then he explained how the Earth-standard time units are built up, sixty seconds to a minute, sixty minutes to an hour, and so on up to a year. The robot, obedient machine that it was, refrained from making sarcastic comments about this inexact and arbitrary system that we have compelled all other races to adopt, at least in their dealings with us. (Why sixty seconds to a minute? Why twenty-four hours to a day? Why not a sensible system built on tens, or logarithms, or something orderly? Ask the Babylonians. I think they invented it.)

When the robot had grasped our time system, Dr. Horkkk moved on to our distance system, blocking out a line one centimeter in length on the vault floor, and then a one-meter line, and finally instructing the robot to visualize a kilometer as a thousand meters. Finally Dr. Horkkk proceeded to define the orbital velocity of this asteroid in terms of kilometers per hour. The robot stepped out of the vault and scanned the heavens for about half a minute, probably measuring parallax effects so it could see for itself how fast the asteroid was traveling through this solar system. Whatever fantastic computing machine is under its skull was quickly able to calculate the orbital velocity of the asteroid in terms of High Ones units of time and distance, and to work out a correlation from that to Earth-standard figures.

The robot said, "I will confirm. The orbital period of this asteroid is one year, six months, five days, three hours, two minutes, and forty-one seconds."

"That's right," said Captain Ludwig.

"Very well," Dr. Horkkk said briskly, as though it were not at all a miracle that this alien machine could learn so fast and that it could calculate orbital periods by a mere glance at the sky. "Now we may proceed. Can you give us an estimate in our terms of the time elapsed since the most recent visit of the Mirt Korp Ahm to this asteroid?"

Again the robot studied the sky—this time, apparently, scanning the stars and measuring the shifts in constellations that had taken place since its last look at the outside world.

Shortly the robot said, "941,285,008 years, two months, twelve days—"

It was like a high-voltage jolt to hear those calm words. The robot confirmed, to superhuman exactness, the calculations of Luna City Observatory. I don't know how many computers Luna City put on that job, or how long they spent at it, but they certainly didn't hand out an instant real-time reply the way Dihn Ruuu had just done. Something like that tends to puncture your pride in human attainments. How much superior to us the High Ones must have been, if they could build a robot that would wait patiently in a cave for 941 million years, still be in prime working order when visitors come, and be capable of tossing off computations of that sort! Zit!

"When was the last time you had contact with the Mirt Korp Ahm?" Pilazinool asked.

"941,285,008 years, two months, twelve—"

"That is, not since the sealing of the vault?"

"Correct. It is my task to await their return."

"They won't return," said Pilazinool. "They haven't been seen in this galaxy for millions of years."

"This is contrary to possibility," Dihn Ruuu replied smoothly. "Their existence could not have ceased. Therefore they must continue to occupy substantial portions of this galaxy. And thus they will return to this place. I must await them."

Dr. Schein cut in, "Do you understand what I mean when I refer to the home world of the Mirt Korp Ahm?"

"The world on which their first evolution occurred," said the robot. "The world which is basic to their history."

"That's it, yes." Dr. Schein leaned forward eagerly. "We've tried to discover this world, but we've had no success. Can you give us information about it? For example: is it located in this galactic cluster?"

"Yes," the robot said.

Dr. Schein looked distressed. He belonged to the school of thought that says the High Ones came from another galaxy. Dr. Horkkk hopped about in triumph. He was one of the first to argue that the High Ones originated right here.

Though shaken, Dr. Schein went on, "Is the star that is the sun of the Mirt Korp Ahm's home world visible from this place?"

"Yes," the robot said.

"I mean, is it *still* visible, after all the time that's passed since you came here?"

"Yes," the robot said.

"Will you point it out for us?" Dr. Schein asked.

I found myself trembling. The others were equally tense. This weird and dreamlike interview with an age-old machine had suddenly erupted into something of incredible importance. Passionate scientific controversies were being settled. The machine would tell us everything. All we had to do was ask! And now it was going to give us the fundamental solution to our quest —the location of the home world of the High Ones.

It stepped out of the vault again for a clear view of the heavens. It looked up.

A minute passed. Two minutes. Three.

No doubt the robot was comparing its recorded

memory of the constellations of 941 million years ago against what it saw now, and making the necessary adjustments that would enable it to trace the wanderings of the High Ones' sun during the elapsed time.

Something was wrong, though. The robot seemed frozen. It scanned the sky, halted, thought, scanned the sky again.

"Perhaps an internal command against revealing the location of the home world has taken control," Dr. Horkkk suggested.

The robot stumbled back into the vault. *Stumbled*, I say. This flawless machine moved with the shambling, staggering gait of someone who's just learned that he's been wiped out by a quick twitch of the stock market, or who's just heard that seven generations of his family were caught in a sunglider accident.

"The star is not there," said the robot in a terrible voice.

"You can't find it?" Dr. Schein asked. "It's not visible from this part of space?"

"It *should* be visible," the robot said. "I have computed its location precisely, and there is no possibility of error. But the star is gone from the sky. I look at the place where I know it must be, and I see only darkness. I detect no energy radiation at all. The star is gone. The star is gone."

"How can a star vanish?" Jan whispered.

"Maybe it went supernova," Saul suggested. "Blew up half a billion years ago—the robot wouldn't have any way of knowing that—"

"The star is gone," said the robot again. The colors of its vision panel dulled in obvious shock and bewilderment. This perfect mechanical brain, with its total grasp on all data, had hit a horrible, numbing inconsistency in its universe—in the most vital part of its universe, too.

We hardly knew what to say. How can you console a robot on the disappearance of its builders' home star?

After a long pause Dihn Ruuu said, "There is no need for me to wait here longer. The star is gone. Where have the Mirt Korp Ahm gone? The Mirt Korp Ahm will never return to this place. The star is gone. The star is gone. It is beyond all understanding, but the star is gone."

fourteen

Dr. Horkkk, always suspicious, went on believing for several days that the robot was lying to us—deliberately concealing the location of the High Ones' home world. The rest of us, led by Pilazinool, felt otherwise.

Pilazinool intuitively thinks the robot is incapable of lying. He argues that it wouldn't have offered to look for its masters' home star unless it really planned to show it to us. And there was no mistaking the despair and confusion that the robot displayed when it was unable to find the star. Dihn Ruuu wasn't designed to show much emotion; but that robot was *shaken* when it came back into the vault.

Where has the star gone?

Maybe Saul's supernova theory is the right one. No one's suggested anything any better, so far. If it's true, it's pretty dismal news for us, since it forecloses our chances of finding and excavating the central planet of the High Ones' empire. A world that's been cooked by a supernova isn't generally of much use to archaeology afterward.

The robot spent the first day and a half after its upsetting discovery at its instruments. It ignored us completely. Standing in the back of the vault, it twiddled dials and scanned data terminals in a sort of panicky quest for information. I think it was looking for recorded messages from others of its kind that might have come in during its hundreds of millions of years of hibernation—something that might explain the inexplicable catastrophe that had befallen the High Ones. But it didn't appear to get much satisfaction.

We kept away from it during this time. Perhaps even a robot can feel grief; and Dihn Ruuu had apparently lost its creators, its masters, its whole reason for existence. It deserved privacy while it found a way of coping with the changes that had befallen its universe.

Then Dihn Ruuu came to us. Leroy Chang saw the robot standing patiently beside the ship, and we went out to it. Consulting the translation machine that it carried, studying the flowing hieroglyphics for a long while, it said at last to us, "Do you have the star travel? The way of going faster than light?"

"We call it ultradrive," Dr. Schein said. "We have it. Yes."

"Good. There is a planet not far from here on which the Mirt Korp Ahm built a large colony. Perhaps you will take me there. I must learn a great deal, and that is the nearest place where I can learn it."

"How far from here?" Pilazinool asked. "In terms of the distance light travels in one year."

Dihn Ruuu paused for one of those astonishing quick calculations. "Thirty-seven times the journey of light in one year."

"Thirty-seven light-years," Dr. Schein repeated. "That won't be too expensive. We can manage it. As soon as the cruiser comes back to check on us—"

"Possibly we would not even have to go there," the robot said. "Have you the way of transmitting messages at faster than light?"

"Yes," said Dr. Schein.

"No," said Dr. Horkkk in the same instant.

Dihn Ruuu swung its gaze from one to the other in bewilderment. "Yes and no? I do not register this."

Dr. Schein laughed. "There *is* a way to communicate at faster-than-light speeds," he said. "But it requires the services of human beings with special gifts. What Dr. Horkkk meant is that we don't have any of those specially gifted people with us now."

"I see," said Dihn Ruuu sadly.

"Even if we did, they probably wouldn't be of much use," Dr. Schein went on. "They can only communicate human-to-human. They wouldn't be able to reach the minds of anyone on a Mirt Korp Ahm planet."

The robot said, "They work by thought amplification, then?"

"That's right. Did the Mirt Korp Ahm have such a way of sending messages?"

"Among themselves, yes," said Dihn Ruuu. "But only protoplasm-life can use the thought amplifiers. Even if other machines of my type still exist in the universe, I could not reach them with the thought amplifier. Only by radio. Which would require thirty-seven years to get to them. I do not wish to wait so long for the answers I need."

Pilazinool said, "We can take you to this other planet, if you have any way of showing us where it is."

"Do you have"—the robot hesitated—"star charts?"

"Sure," Nick Ludwig said. "The whole galaxy's been mapped."

"I will show you, then, on the charts."

Dihn Ruuu looked quickly at the stars, as if taking a fast fix on the constellations, and followed Ludwig into the ship. It moved with great care, perhaps afraid that its bulk and weight would do damage; but we had already tested the sturdiness of the ship on Mirrik, who outweighed even the robot, and had no fears. I wondered, though, what Dihn Ruuu made of the quaint, primitive technology of our ship.

The captain and the robot entered the chart room. Ludwig keyed in the chart tank; its dark surface began to glow, and at a punched command from the captain the ship's computer beamed into the tank an image of the heavens as seen from this asteroid. "Tell us where you want to go," Ludwig said, and Dihn Ruuu pointed to the upper right quadrant of the tank. Ludwig nodded to Webber Fileclerk, who amplified the image; Dihn Ruuu went on indicating quadrants until, three or four step-ups later, a small G-type star with six planets occupied the center of the image.

Fileclerk checked the coordinates, looked it up in the catalog, and found that it was GGC 2787891, also known as McBurney's Star. It had been mapped and surveyed in 2280, but no landings had ever been made on any of its planets.

Nothing surprising about that, of course. There are millions of stars, billions of planets; and the exploration of the galaxy is a long way from complete. We don't share Dihn Ruuu's pathetic belief that there still is a thriving outpost of High Ones in the system of McBurney's Star, but certainly we'll find a major archaeological site there. Which is reason enough for making the trip.

So our expedition, instead of tying us down for two cold and rainy years on Higby V, is turning into a galactic odyssey. First to this asteroid in the system of GGC 1145591, then to McBurney's Star, and who knows where Dihn Ruuu will lead us next? We'll follow. The profits from that mercury mine will take care of the stash problem, and we can worry about detailed archaeological excavation later; these sites won't vanish. Mysteries that we thought forever insoluble are cracking open every day. I mean, here we are *talking* to a robot of the High Ones, asking all kinds of questions about the civilization of its masters and getting answers. And we have the projections from our globe to study, and also the scenes Dihn Ruuu has shown us, and all this machinery in the vault—

The one sad thing is that 408b isn't here to share in the glory and the wonder of it all. Everything we're learning would have been right in its pocket.

We leave here next week—I hope.

When Dr. Schein hired that ultradrive cruiser to bring us here from Higby V last October, he shrewdly hedged his bet. He knew there was a good chance that we wouldn't find the vault in this system, in which case we'd be stranded here with nothing to do and without a TP to summon a ship to pick us up. (Nick Ludwig's ship isn't equipped for ultraspace travel; it's strictly local-haul chartering.) Therefore Dr. Schein arranged that when the cruiser made its return trip through this part of the universe in mid-January, it would detour and come within radio range of us so we could request pickup, if necessary. Buying that detour was expensive, but it put a lid on the possible span of time we could waste here in the event of our pulling a zero in the asteroid belt.

The cruiser will be within radio range in three days. We've already begun broadcasting an all-band pickup signal, just in case they forget to call us. We assume that they'll come down and get us; the big bosses can then negotiate a new ultraspace hop, and off we go to McBurney's Star with Dihn Ruuu as our guide.

Maybe.

Meanwhile we zig along in busywork and routine; we quiz Dihn Ruuu a lot (it's amazing how fast the vocabulary of the robot is growing) and study the machinery in the vault. Now that Dihn Ruuu feels released from its orders by the disappearance of the High Ones' star, and is about to abandon the vault, we have free access to all the gadgetry. Most of it is communications equipment, we now know—not too different in principle, I gather, from our radio setup—but there's also a lot of weaponry. Dihn Ruuu is disarming it now. The robot claims that one small snub-nosed tube sticking out of the side wall is capable of blowing up a

sun at a distance of three light-years. We haven't asked
for a demonstration. The other stuff includes the High
Ones' equivalent of computer banks—more bits of data
recorded on one electron than we get into a whole long
protein chain—and some kind of energy accumulator
that works off starlight and keeps this whole array
powered.

We're just a little worried about the impact of all
these wondrous things on the technology of twenty-
fourth-century Earth, Thhh, Calamor, Dinamon, and
Shilamak. Are we ready for such a horde of High Ones
marvels? Assuming that we can learn to use one one-
thousandth of what we've found in this vault alone,
we're in for a third Industrial Revolution that may
transform society more radically than the steam engine
did in the eighteenth century and the computer in the
twentieth.

As I say, we worry. But it's not up to us to make the
decision; as scientists we have no right to suppress this
find. We're not administrators; we're archaeologists.
We discovered this vault, but we have no responsibility
for the later use or misuse of its contents.

If that sounds like moral wishy-washiness, so be it.
I'd rather be considered wishy-washy than be considered an enemy of knowledge. There are always some
risks in making discoveries; but we'd still be living in
caves and eating our meat raw if somebody, somewhere
along the line, hadn't taken the risk of using his brain.
The big difference here is that these gadgets aren't the
products of slow, patient human toil, developed within
the context of our civilization. They're coming to us
all in one shot as hand-me-downs from a vastly more

mature and complex race. Whether we're capable of handling such things at this stage in our development is yet to be seen.

I repeat: it's not our decision to make. Like Pontius Pilate in that episode in the Near East twenty-four centuries ago, we wash our hands of the matter and accept no blame for what follows. It's our job to find things, and we can't help it if they may be dangerous.

Somehow, though humans are a chimpo lot, I'm not *really* worried. If we haven't succeeded in blowing ourselves up by A.D. 2376, we're probably going to make out all right.

Maybe.

.   .   .

It's January 14, and we've made contact with the cruiser. It'll be landing shortly to pick us up. We won't go immediately to McBurney's Star; the cruiser has its own route to consider. But it will take us (and Ludwig's ship, riding piggyback through ultraspace) to the Aldebaran system, where we can hire an outbound ultradrive ship to get us where we want to go.

The stash from the mercury mine isn't going to cover all this. We'd better come up with a uranium mountain the next time.

.   .   .

Three weeks more have passed since I last put down this cube. It's February 8, and we've just completed a two-day stop at Aldebaran IX. Aldebaran is a big red thing, rather handsome, and it has a pack of planets, several of them colonized. We didn't sightsee. We didn't even land, in fact. Dr. Schein handled the whole thing by radio, arranging for an immediately out-bound ultraspace cruiser to take us to McBurney's Star. We are currently hanging in orbit around Al-debaran IX in Nick Ludwig's ship, waiting for the cruiser to come up and meet us; Nick will once again piggyback his little ship to the cruiser and off we'll go.

This is the first time we've been within reach of a TP communications net since leaving Higby V. So Dr. Schein has sent a full report on our discoveries back to Galaxy Central. I hope everybody is duly croggled by the amazing news.

I wish I had been able to find some excuse for put-ting a skull-to-skull call through to you, Lorie. I want so much to say hello, to tell you what a grand time I'm having, how well we're doing. But you know that private chitchat by TP is prohibitively expensive, especially calling Earth from Aldebaran. My biggest hope is that you've taken part in the relay work on some of our messages and that you know a little of what we're up to.

We leave tonight for McBurney's Star. They cal-culate that we'll be there by the end of the month.

.   .   .

February 30

Right on the old zogger! Here it is the last day of the month, and here we are in orbit around the fourth world of the McBurney system. The ultradrive crew, as usual, didn't stay even for a peek. More fools they.

The view is fabulous. You can sposh your mind

looking at that planet from up here, maybe ten thousand kilometers out in space. The survey team that whizzed through this system in 2280 ought to be resurrected and flayed for failing to spot what's down there on McBurney IV.

It's a complete planet-wide city of the High Ones. *Not* a crumpled ancient relic, but a clean, functioning, perfectly preserved living city. We can see vehicles moving, construction under way, lights going on and off.

What we can't see are any High Ones. We've given the planet a thorough scanning in the hour since we got here, and Dihn Ruuu has had a look with its own scanning equipment, which is superior to ours. We and the robot conclude that McBurney IV is populated by plenty of robots. But if there are any Mirt Korp Ahm down there, they're hidden from view.

Dihn Ruuu, faithful to the end, tells us stubbornly that we're going to find High Ones here. For once we're all in agreement that the robot's wrong. It seems pretty clear to us that McBurney IV is another case of machines in perpetual motion: a planet inhabited by robots with an infinite life-span, waiting as Dihn Ruuu waited for the masters to come back. The masters, though, have been extinct for upward of half a billion years, but since the robots haven't been programmed to consider such a possibility, they just go on and on and on about their chores, keeping the place in good trim, waiting, waiting, waiting some more.

We may be all wrong, naturally. What the zog: we may very well find the High Ones still in business on McBurney IV after all this time. This trip has produced so many surprises already that it isn't safe to rule out any possibility. Nevertheless, I don't really think the Mirt Korp Ahm have survived into our own era. And, as I said many months ago, I'm not sure I'd like to run into them if they did. I don't know what I'd do if I ever found myself face to face with one of the superbeings who built this civilization. Fall flat on my snout and pay homage, I guess. It would be something like meeting a god. My company manners aren't up to meeting gods.

We'll know soon enough, because Dihn Ruuu is now trying to make radio contact with his fellow robots on the planet below, so that they don't blast us out of the sky as we try to land. If all goes well we'll be going into our entry orbit within the hour.

.   .   .

Dihn Ruuu has obtained landing permission for us. We're on our way down.

fifteen

March 10, 2376
McBurney IV

We didn't make a powered landing; the robots wouldn't let us. Communicating with Dihn Ruuu via the ship's radio, they ordered us to cut our engines and submit to proxy control from below.

Mild crisis.

"Like zog I will," Nick Ludwig shouted. "Turn my ship over to unknown alien forces? Risk everybody's life? Either I land this on my own heat or I'm not landing!"

Dihn Ruuu said, "They refuse to permit anything else. You must realize that they have no knowledge of your competence as a pilot. All they see is a strange ship."

Nick blustered some more. Dr. Schein mildly suggested that Nick had better give in. When Nick threatened to turn around and leave, Dr. Schein just as mildly began to talk about breach of contract. He brought up in an oblique way the question of the piece of the mercury mine that we had promised the spaceman, and other likesuch variosities. Nick yielded. He looked like he was ready to go nova, but he yielded.

Some five thousand meters from planetfall he cut the engines and we slipped back into a parking orbit. Then the robots grabbed us from below. As if yanking on us with a giant magnet, they pulled us out of orbit and guided us down. We were completely inertialess: just floating toward McBurney IV under no means of acceleration, but making a pretty good velocity. Nick Ludwig invited us up front to look at his instruments. I've never seen a man more perplexed. "What are they going to do?" he asked. "Catch us in a net? We're building up speed at what looks like a one-g acceleration, but where's the acceleration? *Where are the laws of physics?*"

Repealed, I guess. All the tonnage of our ship was nothing more than a straw on the wind, a sliver of iron in a magnetic field. We went down and down and down in a dreamy way and came to rest, gently, easily, in the precise center of a huge bullseye target where we were surrounded by gaunt, spidery rings of instruments, stretching away for hundreds of meters on every side. Golden loops and coils and towers and crosshatched antennae hemmed us in: the equipment that had plucked us from the sky and set us down, no doubt. Nick Ludwig, pale and dazed, stared at all this in distress. It was an article of faith for poor Nick that planetary landings were to be made according to the principles of Newton, with thrust balancing pull, deceleration canceling acceleration. But this landing was pure magic. Inertialess acceleration indeed!

The atmosphere of McBurney IV tested out as breathable, maybe, but risky on account of a heavy carbon dioxide concentration and some whiffs of something hexafluoride. So we went outside in breathing-suits, with Dihn Ruuu leading the way. The gravity was a bit more than Earthnorm; the weather was hot.

A dozen robots of Dihn Ruuu's general shape greeted us. Clustered about us, like vast walking statues. Peered at us, sniffed us, touched us. Communicated with one another about us, via an audio channel we could not pick up.

"What are they saying?" I asked Dihn Ruuu. "Do the Mirt Korp Ahm still occupy this planet?"

"I have not yet been able to obtain information on that subject," said the robot.

"Why are they so excited, then?"

"They have never seen protoplasmic life before," Dihn Ruuu replied. "These are machines that were created by other machines. They are captured by you."

"Captivated," I corrected.

Dihn Ruuu didn't acknowledge the correction. Our robot had hooked itself into the conversation and had ceased to take notice of us. For perhaps five minutes the delegation of metal beings conferred earnestly. Pilazinool seemed to be getting more than his share of attention; I realized finally that the High Ones robots thought that he was *our* robot, since so much of his body was nonorganic, and they were trying to draw him into the discussion. Dihn Ruuu explained, I think.

Vehicles appeared. Six long, slim aircars made of green plastic came whistling down, and from their bellies descended metal scoops, onto which we moved at the instructions of Dihn Ruuu. Up we went, into the aircars, and away, flying at a height of perhaps a hundred meters. To the city.

The city was everywhere. Once we were beyond the concentric rings of the spaceport and its intricate landing devices, we were in the city. It resembled in general look the High Ones cities we had seen on our globe, but in actual point of detail there were very few correspondences at all. The buildings did not dangle; each was firmly rooted, although there were so many levels that we had difficulty tracing any one row of buildings through the maze. The design of each building was different from those we had seen earlier; these were sleek pyramid-shaped structures, mostly, whose surfaces glowed with a soft inner light. I saw no windows.

We were taken to a particularly large pyramid and left by ourselves in a spherical room of colossal size. Little blobs of golden light drifted freely near the ceiling. Abstract decorative patterns, red streaks and purple dots and blue spirals, rotated dizzyingly in panels on the walls. There was nothing to sit on except the floor, which was carpeted in something soft and spongy and seemingly alive, for it wriggled and writhed whenever someone put his weight on it. All the robots left us. Including Dihn Ruuu, our one link to the real universe, our guide, our interpreter.

Two hours passed, and then two hours more.

We hardly spoke. We sat or stood or sprawled

around the great room, puzzled, ill at ease, off guard, baffled into a state of total spinlessness. This episode had taken on all the qualities of a dream: our floating descent, the jostling and pinching given us by the towering robots, our inability to communicate with anyone, the eerie silence, the strangeness of the city, the unreality of this bare cavernous room in which we now found ourselves . . . prisoners.

Conversation, such as it was, tended to be made up mostly of phrases like:

"Where are we?"

"What does it all mean?"

"How long will they keep us here?"

"Where are the High Ones?"

"Are there any High Ones?"

"Why doesn't Dihn Ruuu come back?"

"Whose pocket are we in?"

"What's the whole giboo about?"

Since we had no answers to any of these questions, conversations that began with them tended to be rather brief. By the end of the second hour we had exhausted most immediate themes of this sort and had lapsed into silence all around. Mirrik and Kelly, as usual, were fairly cheerful; Dr. Horkkk sat by himself in a kind of black meditation, all his legs tightly crossed; Pilazinool unscrewed limbs; Dr. Schein wore a frown that deepened and deepened, as though he were having a great many second thoughts all at once; Leroy Chang skulked; Saul Shahmoon seemed to be asleep, possibly dreaming about the postage stamps of McBurney IV; Nick Ludwig paced like a caged beast; Jan and I sat close together, and occasionally one of us flashed a quick nervous grin at the other. We tried not to show our fear; but, after all, this was no dream.

In the third hour we began to wonder when, if ever, the robots planned to let us out. Or feed us. We had a couple of days' supply of food tablets, but for all we knew we'd be left here two or three months before anyone considered our needs. We had hardly any supply of water. There weren't any hygienic facilities in here either.

It was the longest afternoon of my life, I think. Here we were in the midst of an incredible city of an ancient civilization—and unable to see a thing, unsure of what was in store.

Finally a place in the wall below one of the stripe-and-dot panels began to swell and pucker; it popped open and Dihn Ruuu stepped through. I could see a couple of the other robots lurking just beyond the opening. Dihn Ruuu moved slowly to the center of the room and swiveled to scan us all.

"The Mirt Korp Ahm," the robot announced solemnly, "no longer inhabit the present planet. I have learned that this outpost was abandoned by them 84,005,675 years ago, and is currently occupied only by the Dihn Ruuu, that is to say, the Machines To Serve."

The calm words, delivered in that weird metallic imitation of my own voice, hit us with tremendous impact.

We weren't amazed to find that there were no High Ones here, just a population of self-sufficient, virtually immortal robots. But to learn that the High Ones had abandoned McBurney IV only some eighty-four million years ago—!

Funny how your perspective changes. On Earth eighty-four million years ago the dinosaurs still went stumbling around, and the only mammals that existed were little ratty things with long noses and sharp teeth. Nor had intelligent life evolved on any of the other planets of our galaxy that currently have it, such as Shilamak, Dinamon, or Thhh. So by any human perspective, eighty-four million years ago is pre-pre-pre-pre-historic.

Yet I said *only* eighty-four million years. And I wasn't jesting.

Up to this point all archaeological evidence had indicated, as I'm sure I've told you, that the High Ones had mysteriously disappeared from our galaxy 850 million years ago. No trace of them more recent than that had ever been found. On that scale, eighty-four million years ago was practically last week. With one brief statement Dihn Ruuu had lopped away 90 percent of the time-span since the vanishing of the High Ones.

The implications of the robot's statement staggered us. Seemingly we would have to rethink our entire outlook on the High Ones and their place in the sequence of time. A dozen questions jiggled my brain at once, and it must have been the same for everyone else. But before we could get anything out, Dihn Ruuu iced us on all wavelengths with a far more sposhing statement.

Like a college professor reading off routine announcements at the beginning of class, Dihn Ruuu went on, "It is with great pleasure that I state that the home world of the Mirt Korp Ahm does in fact still exist, and neither it nor its star have been destroyed, despite the impossibility of locating them that I experienced. According to communications received on this planet 13,595,486 years ago, the Mirt Korp Ahm embarked on a project at that time for the transformation of their home system into an enclosed sphere permitting full utilization of the solar energy. An uninhabited planet of the system was used as the source of mass for this project. The enterprise was successfully completed within a period of 150 years after receipt of first notice here. Thereafter, naturally, the home star of the Mirt Korp Ahm ceased to be detectible by conventional optical means."

I pondered the meaning of that set of cloudy phrases without much immediate success. But to Saul Shahmoon the robot's explanation was lucidity itself.

"Of course!" Saul cried. "A Dyson sphere!"

Taking no notice of the interruption, Dihn Ruuu sailed serenely onward. "No communications have been received from the home world since the completion of the enclosure project," the robot said. "However, there is every reason to believe that the Mirt Korp Ahm continue to inhabit their original solar system. Inasmuch as my own responsibilities have been terminated, I propose to journey at once to that system and request reassignment. It would please me if you were to accompany me there."

＊   ＊   ＊

Time out for explanations. I needed some myself, at this point.

A Dyson sphere, according to Saul, is a concept first put forth by an American physicist, Freeman Dyson, some time in the early years of the Energy Revolution. Dyson lived in the middle of the twentieth century, after the harnessing of atomic energy but before the colonization of Earth's surrounding planets.

Dyson's main point was that in its natural state a solar system is a terribly wasteful thing. The central sun, surrounded by a handful of planets, sends most of its energy shooting uselessly off into space. The planets are too widely separated to intercept more than a small fraction of the energy the sun generates; and therefore the sun's output speeds away in all directions, radiating so intensely in the visible spectrum alone that its light can be seen thousands of light-years away. This has the esthetic advantage of producing lovely starry nights on distant worlds, but otherwise has little to commend it.

A really thrifty civilization, Dyson said, would catch all of its sun's energy before it was squandered. One way to do it, he suggested, was to demolish Jupiter and use its mass to build a shell surrounding the sun at approximately the distance of Earth's orbit from the center of the solar system. Smashing up the biggest planet and rearranging its pieces this way would take a fair amount of energy all by itself: roughly as much as the sun's total output for eight hundred years. But once the job was finished, the shell would intercept every photon of energy coming from the sun; this could be put to use as an all-purpose power source.

Mankind would cease to live on the Earth, which even in his time was a pretty small and crowded place, and unsatisfactory in terms of application of solar energy, since at any given time half of it is receiving no solar radiation at all. Instead we would take up residence on the inner surface of the artificial sphere. Not only would every point on that surface have full access to sunlight at every moment, but the surface area of the sphere would be about one billion times greater than the surface area of the Earth. Splicing in all the plus factors, we'd find that the sphere could comfortably support a human population of 3×10^{23} individuals, which is to say a good many sextillion or septillion people—work out the exponents yourself. Anyway, it would be a gigantic number. Let's see: Earth has thirteen billion people now, which is 13×10^9, and things are pretty crowded, and this would be a population increase of 10^{14}, so . . . It gives you the dizzies, eh?

Dyson thought that any intelligent species would be capable of converting its home world into such a sphere within two or three thousand years after it entered the industrial age. So we ought to be able to do it about 4000 A.D. However, it must be a tougher trick in practice than in theory, if the Mirt Korp Ahm, whom we know were at the stage of galactic travel 1.1 billion years ago, waited until a mere thirteen *million* years ago to do it. Or did they just not bother to get around to it any earlier?

A Dyson sphere would not, of course, show up on optical telescopes, since all of the sun's light output is trapped inside the sphere. That explains Dihn Ruuu's failure to see the star when he looked for it in the sky. Nevertheless, even a Dyson-sphere civilization would be unable to make use of *all* the energy that was available to it, and would have to get rid of some of it in the form of heat, that is to say, infrared radiation. Dyson suggested that the sphere would have a surface temperature of 200° to 300° K., and would be emitting plentiful radiation in the far infrared wavelengths. This, of course, could be detected easily by outside observers.

Dihn Ruuu could stop grieving, then. The home star of his creators had neither burned out nor blown up. It was still there—under wraps, so to speak.

.   .   .

Small surprises eclipse big miracles. Old Paradoxian proverb, just invented by your humble servant. Dihn Ruuu had thrown so much astonishing news at us in a dozen sentences that for a moment, in the excitement of the Dyson-sphere discussion, we forgot to get excited over the real orbit-smasher, which was . . .

That the High Ones possibly weren't extinct at all. . . .

And that Dihn Ruuu was inviting us to help him pay a call on them.

Wonders were multiplying too swiftly.

Of course, Dihn Ruuu's guess that the High Ones were still alive was *only* a guess. The McBurney IV robots had heard neither beep nor plink from the Mirt Korp Ahm in thirteen million years, and it's dangerous to think of thirteen million years as anything but a zog of a long time. On the other hand, we were accustomed to thinking of the High Ones as beings buried a billion years in the past; if they had survived until thirteen million years ago, it was a reasonable bet that they still existed. On the third hand—

We did a lot of talking all at once, shouting out

theories, disputations, suppositions, postulates, hypotheses, and even some plain old guesses. Nobody could hear anybody else in the uproar, until suddenly one voice cut across all the rest:

"Help!"

We fell silent and looked around.

"Who called for help?" Dr. Schein asked.

"I did," Pilazinool said in a small voice. "I finally did it."

He finally had. During our excited outburst, the Shilamakka had given way to his old nervous habit of unfastening hands and feet and limbs, and this time, in a kind of supreme act of self-multilation, he had contrived to unscrew everything at once, arms and legs. Don't ask me how. I guess he was simultaneously unscrewing his right arm with his left, and his left with his right; however it happened, he had stripped himself down to a bare torso and was looking piteously at his heap of discarded limbs, unable to start assembling himself again. His expression of bewilderment was so intense that I was afraid something was seriously wrong. But then Dr. Schein began to laugh, and Mirrik snorted, and Kelly picked up one of Pilazinool's arms and put it in place, whereupon Pilazinool began hastily and in huge embarrassment to get the rest of himself attached.

The interruption was just what we needed. We were calm again.

Dr. Schein said quietly, "Dihn Ruuu asks us to follow him to the planet of the High Ones. I'll call for a vote. All in favor—?"

Guess how *that* vote turned out.

But certain practical difficulties keep us from blasting off at once for Mirt, which is what the home world of the High Ones is called. Such as the fact that Mirt is seventy-eight light-years from McBurney IV, and the only transportation available to us at the moment is Nick Ludwig's ship, which can't travel at ultradrive speeds. If we set out tomorrow for Mirt in Nick's ship, I'd celebrate my hundredth birthday before we got there.

So we have to go through the cumbersome business of waiting for our ultradrive cruiser to come back this way on the prearranged checkup flight. That'll be a month from now. And then to charter a flight to Mirt, if we have the stash to swing it.

Actually, that isn't too bad. It gives us some time to explore McBurney IV before we rush off to the next wonderworld. It's unhealthy to gulp down a surfeit of miracles; gives one indigestion of the imagination. Whole careers could be spent just in this one place. Not archaeological careers, I suppose; the story of the High Ones has exploded out of archaeology now. But McBurney IV holds a million times as much to dazzle us as did the cave on the asteroid in the 1145591 system; and we thought *that* was a high-spectrum load!

The robots here have been very cooperative. Dihn Ruuu explained to them that we were stranded here until our ultraspace ship picked us up, and they accepted that. Whereupon we became honored guests and tourists, instead of prisoners. For the past week we've been using the ship as our base, and taking off each day on a sightseeing trip through the Mirt Korp Ahm's outpost here.

It's clear now why this place is so different, architecturally, from what we saw in our globe. The cities shown by the globe were a billion years old. McBurney IV was still inhabited by the Mirt Korp Ahm less than a hundred million years ago. Even among so conservative a race as the High Ones, architectural styles do change in hundreds of millions of years. Dangling cities went out of fashion here.

We are only skimming the surface of this world of course. Hairy primitives that we are, we can hardly begin to understand what we see. The power accumulators, draining energy from McBurney's Star and socking it away underground. The master brain centers that run the transit systems. The automatic repair mechanisms that come scuttling out to fix any mechanical difficulty instantly. The great scanners that tirelessly search the sky for a hint of a signal from the Mirt Korp Ahm—a signal that never comes, alas! The robots themselves, the Dihn Ruuu, self-lubricating, self-repairing, seemingly immortal. The aircars: do they run on antigravity engines? Everything dazzles and bewilders.

Fantastic as their cities are, though, the Mirt Korp Ahm aren't really a billion years ahead of us in technological development. Considering the head start they had, the High Ones actually seem a little backward, as though consciously or otherwise they froze their culture at this level long ago. I mean, this supercivilization of theirs is just about what I'd expect Earth to have in, say, the year 10,000, if I projected our technological growth forward on the same curve as it's been following since about A.D. 1700. But it's not what I'd expect Earth to have in the year 1,000,-002,376. Not by plenty.

I don't think I can even imagine what a culture that's been developing steadily for a billion years *ought* to be like. Disembodied electrical essences, maybe. Ghostly creatures flitting in and out of the eighth, ninth, and tenth dimensions. Cosmic minds that know all, perceive all, understand all.

Maybe I'm being unfair to the Mirt Korp Ahm. Perhaps the growth curve of our technology in the years 1700-2300 was wildly atypical; perhaps the growth curve of *any* civilization inevitably flattens out once it reaches a certain level. I can't help feeling that the Mirt Korp Ahm should have gone farther than they did, with all the time they had to evolve, but possibly they bucked up against the absolute limits of ingenuity and went static. Possibly the same thing will happen to us, two or three thousand years up the line. I wonder.

In any case, we're having a glorious time, in an unreal and dreamy way. Did any of this seem probable when we set out to grub in the dirt on Higby V?

.   .   .

Same cube, four days later. Much confusion.

Scene: our ship. Hour: late. Cast of characters: me, Jan, Pilazinool. Everyone else asleep.

Mysterious bleeping sounds emerge from ship's audio system. Who calls us here? Local robots tuning in on our channel? Unlikely. Maybe some Earth ship calling. No Earth ships within a dozen light-years, at least. None expected here for several weeks. What spins? Pilazinool says, unworried, "Tom, see what's happening over there."

Tom Rice, Boy Radioman, goes to audio panel, ponders its intricacy a moment, taps buttons and spins dials, meanwhile making official-sounding noises like, "Come in, come in, I'm not reading you, come in." And so forth. Simultaneously does his best to improve reception so that unknown message from space can be detected. Also switches on recorder, in case anything important is arriving, though he knows innate improbability that someone would call us *here*.

Out of the receptor comes male human voice, reciting the call numbers of our ship. "Confirm," voice says. "Do you read me?" it inquires.

"I read you," I say, feeling like a minor character in a bad tridim film. "Who's calling? What's going on?"

"Ultradrive cruiser *Pride of Space*, Commander Leon Leonidas, calling Captain Nicholas Ludwig."

"Ludwig's asleep," I reply. "So's just about everybody else. My name's Tom Rice, and I don't really have much authority, but—"

Jan, coming over to listen, nudges me and whispers, "Maybe they're in distress, Tom!"

Thought seems logical. Unscheduled arrival of unknown ultradrive cruiser—emergency landing, maybe—difficulties on board—

I say, "Are you in trouble, *Pride of Space*?"

"We aren't. You are. We have orders from Galaxy Central to place you under arrest."

It dawns on me that the conversation is not going well.

I boost the gain so Pilazinool can catch what's being said.

"Arrest?" I repeat loudly. "There's some mistake. We're an archaeological expedition conducting research in—"

"Exactly. We have instructions to pick up a team of eleven archaeologists and bring the bunch of you back to Galaxy Central at once. I advise cooperation. We're right upstairs, in orbit around McBurney IV, and we want you to wrap up your work within two hours and get up here into a matching orbit so we can bring you on board. If you don't cooperate, I'm afraid we'll have to come down and get you. Please take down the following orbital coordinates—"

"Wait," I say. "I've got to notify the others. I don't understand anything of what's going on."

Jan is already scurrying toward the cabins to wake people up. Pilazinool has removed several limbs. The voice out of the receptors, sounding terribly calm and very, very military, asks me to find one of my superiors and put him on the line right away. I stammer something apologetic and ask my caller to wait.

Dr. Schein, looking sleepy and grim, stumbles into the room.

"It's a Navy ultradrive ship," I say. "Sent here by Galaxy Central to arrest us. We've got two hours to get off this planet and turn ourselves in."

Dr. Schein makes a face of disgust, squinting eyes, clamping lips. Goes to audio. "Hello," he says. "Schein speaking. What's all this nonsense about?"

Not a good approach. Calm military voice gets icier, explains all over again that our galactic odyssey is at its end. By now everybody else has crowded into the cabin. Nick Ludwig, yawning, demands to know the story. I tell him. Ludwig chews on knuckles and groans. Steen Steen says, "They can't make us do anything. We're safe here. If they try to land without permission, the robots will blow them up."

Jan tells him patiently, "We'd be crazy to defy a Navy ship. Anyway, what good would it do? We're stuck here until we get ultradrive transport out."

Dr. Schein, meanwhile, is speaking in low, earnest voice to *Pride of Space*. Impossible to hear conversation because of general hubbub. When he turns away from audio, he looks old, gray, beaten.

"Somebody go and find Dihn Ruuu," he says. "We've got to leave. Galaxy Central has its clamps on us at last."

"Don't give in!" Steen Steen cries. "We're free agents! The era of slavery is over!"

Dr. Schein ignores him. "Nick," he says, "get the ship ready. We're going upstairs."

.   .   .

Dihn Ruuu arrived; we explained things; and the robot arranged for our quick exit from McBurney IV. We left as we had come, with our engines cut off, and went eerily whistling upward in the grip of the same powerful force that had drawn us down. The robots who were controlling our ascent inserted us neatly into the orbit of the *Pride of Space* and let go; we switched to our own power, matched velocities with the big starship, and let ourselves be pulled into the custody of the Galaxy Central Navy. The sight of Dihn Ruuu brought the whole crew out to gape, up to and including the commander.

Commander Leonidas turned out to be a crisp, dapper little man of about fifty, with pale blue eyes and a warm, sympathetic nature. He made it very clear as soon as we were on board that he was simply doing his job, nothing personal in it.

"I've never had to arrest archaeologists before. What were you people doing—smuggling on the side?"

"We have done nothing but legitimate research!" snapped Dr. Horkkk, furious as always.

"Well, maybe so," Commander Leonidas said, shrugging. "But somebody at Galaxy Central is upset about you. Pick you up at once, that's what I was told! No delay! Tolerate no opposition! As if I was catching a bunch of sposhing mutineers."

"What you are doing," said Dr. Horkkk in his thinnest and nastiest of voices, "is preventing us from completing one of the greatest scientific accomplishments of the past ten thousand years."

"Really, now? I hadn't realized—"

"By your interference," Dr. Horkkk went on, "you interrupt our journey just as we are about to solve the final mystery of the Mirt Korp Ahm, the High Ones, as you call them. You snatch us away at the moment of greatest accomplishment. The stupidity of the military mind is a universal curse that—"

Commander Leonidas' sunny expression was beginning to darken, and I could see that if Dr. Horkkk kept it up, we'd finish the voyage in irons. Mirrik and Pilazinool saw it too, and tactfully moved in on Dr.

Horkkk from opposite sides, pinning him between them and shutting him up.

Absolute dejection was what we all felt. We couldn't understand what Galaxy Central was up to, but it was utterly clear that we were going to be hauled away from our work, forced to defend our actions before the bureaucrats, and probably prevented permanently from seeing the planet of the High Ones. By the time we got everything straightened out, some other expedition would have been assigned to that plum.

The Commander produced a little data viewer and said, "If you don't mind, I'd like to take a personnel inventory. As I call your name, would you kindly acknowledge? Dr. Milton Schein?"

"Yes."

"Pilazinool of Shilamak?"

"Yes."

He went right through the list. Naturally, 408b of Bellatrix XIV did not reply. On the other hand, one robot of alien design had been added to the group but wasn't on Commander Leonidas' roster. Dr. Schein explained impatiently that 408b had been killed in an accident last December, that the robot was a High Ones product that we had picked up at the same time, and that Galaxy Central knew all this anyway, since he had passed it along via TP during our stop at Aldebaran IX.

"Aldebaran IX?" Commander Leonidas repeated blankly. "Your dossier doesn't include any messages sent from Aldebaran IX."

"In early February," said Dr. Schein. "We went

there after leaving the asteroid in the 1145591 system where—"

"Hold it," the Navy man cut in. "Galaxy Central asserts that you were last heard from on a planet called Higby V, where you're supposed to be conducting an excavation of some old ruins. You left Higby V without authorization and disappeared. That was in violation of your agreement with Galaxy Central, and therefore—"

Dr. Schein broke in, "We left Higby V to go to 1145591, and from there we went to Aldebaran IX, where I sent a complete TP report to Galaxy Central."

"Not as far as anyone told me, Doctor."

"There's been a mistake," Dr. Schein suggested. "A computer error—a data transposition—a dropped bit. This whole arrest order must be erroneous."

Commander Leonidas looked troubled. Also puzzled.

Pilazinool said quietly, "Commander, precisely how did you trace us to McBurney IV?"

"I didn't trace you anywhere. I was ordered to come here and pick you up. Presumably Galaxy Central knew you were here."

"Galaxy Central did know," said Pilazinool, "because Dr. Schein sent word from Aldebaran that we were coming here. At the same time, he received full authorization from Galaxy Central to make this trip. If Galaxy Central lost track of us after Higby V, as you claim it says, how could Galaxy Central possibly know we had gone to McBurney's Star?"

Commander Leonidas had to admit the logic of that. He fumbled through the text of his arrest order, looking for a solution to the inconsistency, and didn't find one. Leave it to the galactic bureaucracy: the right hands know not what the left hands are doing. Or tentacles, as the case may be.

Pilazinool said, "Do you have TP personnel on this ship?"

"Yes," said Commander Leonidas.

"I think," said Pilazinool, "you'd do well to put through a call to someone at Galaxy Central right now and get things straightened out."

"That might be a good idea," the Commander agreed.

Getting anything straightened out with Galaxy Central is a slow business. Everybody important went off to the TP section, and a few frantic hours followed. What finally emerged was the realization that one officious vidj at Galaxy Central, remembering that we had promised to ship the globe there as part of the agreement letting us go on to 1145591, realized the globe hadn't showed up. He called Higby V and found that we were gone, globe and all. If he had bothered to run a routine data-tank recap, he'd have found that we had sent word from Aldebaran that it had been necessary to take the globe with us. Instead, jumping two or three notches in the sequence of events, this particular blenking feeb had cleverly ordered a computer search of all ultraspace transit vouchers for the past six months, in order to find us, and thus turned up the fact that we had gone from 1145591 to Aldebaran and from Aldebaran to McBurney's Star. We had Galaxy Central's permission to do all this, but he didn't check the correspondence tank, just the transit data. Whereupon this dreary zoob erroneously concluded that we were unlawfully running all over space on Galaxy Central's thumb, as well as taking valuable property in defiance of an agreement, and decided to put a stop to this squandering of public stash by arresting us instantly. Hence the order to Commander Leonidas to put the yank on us at McBurney IV.

I repeat all this devious foolishness because it gives a beautiful illustration of how catastrophes can sometimes turn out pretty well. By the time Dr. Schein got finished making TP calls to Galaxy Central, you see, he had accomplished more than getting that dumb arrest order blotted. He had explained, to someone *very* high in the hierarchy, all about Dihn Ruuu, the Mirt Korp Ahm, and the hidden world of Mirt. And, since Commander Leonidas and his ultraspace cruiser are now conveniently in orbit around McBurney IV, it will not be necessary for us to wait weeks and weeks to arrange our transport to Mirt.

Commander Leonidas will take us there.

We leave tomorrow—for the home planet of the High Ones.

sixteen

Now I know that I have been talking only to myself all the time I've been dictating these cubes. Lorie will never play them. What I have been composing over these past nine months, imagining I was writing letters to my sister on Earth, is actually a memoir of my own adventures, a diary for my own amusement.

In that case, I suppose I should complete the record by setting down the outcome of this phase of the story. The story doesn't end here; it's really only beginning. What is yet to come is the real research, the sorting out of the immense treasury of new knowledge that we've acquired. But that promises to be at once more exciting and less dramatic, if I follow what I'm trying to say. I mean, the next phase of discovery won't unfold in such a fantastic rush of events—I hope.

.   .   .

The *Pride of Space* brought us to Mirt by early April. Dihn Ruuu, Commander Leonidas, and Nick Ludwig plotted our course together, after sighting the hidden star by infrared. Cautiously the cruiser pulled up ten light-minutes away from the dark shell that houses the High Ones. There was no telling what defensive weapons might go into action against a ship that came closer without permission.

The shell that is Mirt is the most awesome thing I have ever seen. From a distance of ten light-minutes it appears to fill half the sky, a great dark curving shield with a diameter greater than that of Earth's whole orbit. Even while Saul had been explaining Dyson spheres to us, I hadn't really considered in serious practical terms what it means to build a sphere big enough to contain a sun. I know now.

Dihn Ruuu, using High Ones broadcast equipment acquired on McBurney IV, put through a signal to Mirt and requested entry permission for us. The robot needed three and a half hours to get its message across. Because of our distance from the sphere, there had to be a lag of ten minutes betwen the time any audio signal was transmitted and the time it was received, but this alone couldn't account for Dihn Ruuu's seeming difficulties in persuading Mirt to let us in. The incomprehensible exchanges of alien words went on and on.

Finally Dihn Ruuu rose and told us, "It is done. They will admit us."

I asked, "Were you having trouble communicating with them because of changes in the language?"

"The language of the Mirt Korp Ahm," said the robot coolly, "is not susceptible to change."

"Not *ever*? Not even over millions of years?"

"Not a syllable has altered since I was manufactured."

"That's incredible," I said. "That a language won't change at all in almost a billion years."

"The Mirt Korp Ahm have never admired continuous evolution," said Dihn Ruuu. "They seek perfection, and, when they have attained it, seek no more."

"But how can they tell when they've attained it?"

"They can tell."

"And then they stop trying to improve anything?"

"It is the difference, Tom, between your race and the one I serve. From what I have seen of you, I realize that you Earthfolk are never satisfied; by definition, you will never be satisfied. You are perpetual seekers. The Mirt Korp Ahm are capable of contentment when they reach perfection in any endeavor. You would try to improve on perfection itself."

I saw now why the 250 million years of our archaeological record of the High Ones had registered so little change. And why they had endured across a billion years.

A supercivilization, yes. But a supercivilization of supertortoises . . . never sticking out their necks. Achieving greatness and pulling into their shells. *Literally* building a shell around their own sun.

Jan said, "If the Mirt Korp Ahm aren't seekers, why did they colonize half the galaxy?"

"It was," said Dihn Ruuu, "a long time ago, when there still was much for them to learn. As you see, the colonies were long ago disbanded. The Mirt Korp

Ahm reversed their outward thrust and returned to their native planet."

Dr. Schein broke in. "Just now, when you were calling Mirt—did you speak with any Mirt Korp Ahm?"

"I spoke only with my own kind," said the robot.

"But the Mirt Korp Ahm—do they still survive inside the shell? Or are we heading for another world of robots?"

"I do not know," Dihn Ruuu said. "Something strange has happened, I fear. But they would not give me any information about the Mirt Korp Ahm."

.   .   .

We approached the shell of Mirt and it opened for us. A huge hinged section of the dark, dully gleaming sphere swung out, a section at least the size of Ohio, and we plunged through, not under our own power but once again in the grip of the force with which the planets of the Mirt Korp Ahm control spaceships.

It was our good luck to be aboard a military vessel, not an ordinary passenger-and-freight ultradrive cruiser; thus our ship was equipped with viewscreens and we were able to watch our own entry into the sphere of Mirt. We saw the vast outer skin of the shell, and the colossal hinged gateway, and the hint of a bright gleam within. Then we sped into the sphere, into a dazzling realm of light. In the center of everything was the sun, white, no larger than Earth's own star, sending forth radiation that danced and glittered over the fantastic sprawl of the sphere's inner surface.

A single giant city covered that surface. Spidery

towers stabbed hundreds of meters into the sky—solar energy accumulators, I learned later. Bright blue points of flame blazed here; giant booms swung and pivoted there; highways sparkled like tracks of fire; somber pyramids of black metal occupied immense areas. Everything seemed in motion, expanding, conquering adjoining territory, sucking in life and power, growing, throbbing. It was not what I expected the world of the conservative, progress-hating Mirt Korp Ahm to resemble.

But were there in fact any Mirt Korp Ahm here?

Or were the robots of the High Ones keeping this unbelievable world alive, obediently carrying on the functions and traditions of their extinct creators?

We landed, coming down in a target area ten times as large as the one on McBurney IV, and bordered by pulsating generators and accumulators of terrifying complexity and size. Robots who might have been the twins of our Dihn Ruuu greeted us. We were taken from our ship, placed aboard a vehicle shaped like a teardrop of amber, and our tour began.

"An extended recitation of wonders," according to the Paradoxians, "makes the merely commonplace seem noble and strange." Perhaps so. I will offer no catalog of the miracles of Mirt. Why wrestle into words what everyone will see so vividly in the tridim images? We viewed all the spendor of a billion-year-old civilization; let that bald statement be enough. Our robot hosts were eager to reveal everything. And, like wanderers in a dream, we who had known the High Ones only by the scraps and potsherds of the inconceivably remote past now journeyed—unbelievably, and only half believing—through the living heart of this vanished empire.

"Where are the Mirt Korp Ahm themselves?" we kept asking. "Do they still exist?"

"They still exist," Dihn Ruuu told us at last, having learned it from the other robots. "But they have changed. They are no longer as I knew them."

"Where are they?"

"They receive special care."

"When will we see them?"

"In time," said the robot. "At the proper moment."

We doubted that. We all were sure that the High Ones had died out long ago; and that the robots, unwilling to accept the hard truth of that, had been living a weird pretense, masterless for millions of years. We were wrong. In their own good time the robots allowed us to meet the Mirt Korp Ahm. It was on the ninth day of our visit. A vehicle of a kind we had not used before called for us and took us down a sloping track into the depths of the sphere, a dozen levels beneath the surface, into a cool green world of silence, where floating globes of light drifted ahead of us down intricate webworks of corridors.

Dihn Ruuu said, "The current Mirt Korp Ahm population of Mirt, I have been told, is 4,852. There has been no significant change in that figure in the past hundred thousand years. The last actual death was recorded here 38,551 years ago."

"And the last birth?" Mirrik asked.

Dihn Ruuu stared at him a long moment and replied, "Approximately four million years ago." After that their fertility was exhausted."

I tried to comprehend the nature of a race whose last baby had been born in the epoch of the subhuman man-apes, whose last death had occurred in the time of the cave painters.

A sliding panel rolled back and we peered through a thick crystal wall at a member of the Mirt Korp Ahm.

In a cavernous six-sided room that reminded me of the rock vault in which we had found Dihn Ruuu, a cluster of massive machinery converged on a cup-shaped couch of glossy blue metal. Enthroned on the couch sat a being of great size, perhaps twice the size of a human, dome-headed, four-armed, covered with scales, indeed a High One such as we had seen in the projections of the globe.

Life-support mechanisms surrounded and practically engulfed it. A dozen small cubical structures were fastened to its limbs; a complex device was strapped about its chest; wires ran from its skull, its body, its wrists. This entire immense room was a nest of equipment that served to sustain the flicker of life in this creature, to nourish it and keep its organs pumping and drain off the poisons of age.

For this High One was old. Hideously, frighteningly old.

Its body was wrinkled and pouchy; its scales no longer overlapped, but had spread apart to show folds of soft grayish skin, and in places the scales had flaked off altogether; the eyes were dull; the expression was slack.

The High One did not move. It gave no indication that it was aware of us. It might have been a waxen image of itself, except for the faint sign of the rise and fall of its breath. Locked within its cradle of cables and conduits and muscle-stimulators and energizers, the prisoner of its own hunger to survive, it seemed lost in a dream of bygone thousands of centuries. We stared at it as if it were a royal mummy come to life, or the last of the dinosaurs.

Commander Leonidas had brought one of his TP people along from the ship. "Can you read it?" Leonidas asked. "Do you pick anything up?"

TPs are not ordinarily supposed to be able to communicate with nonhuman species. But sometimes an alien race carries a strong residual load of latent TP —maybe not strong enough to let members of that race read each other, but enough so that a good Earth TP can pick up stray scraps of thought. Nothing coherent, just flickering impressions rather than full phrases. The TP with us, a man named Davis, pressed close against the crystal wall, closed his eyes, entered into deep concentration. When he turned away moments later, his face was pale and furrowed in disgust.

"A vegetable," Davis said softly. "The mind of a vegetable . . . but an insane vegetable."

"Ozymandias," Mirrik murmured. "Look on my works, ye Mighty, and despair."

Dihn Ruuu said, "They are all like that. Their bodies will endure until the end of time, perhaps. But their minds . . . their minds . . ."

"More dead than alive," Dr. Schein said. "And yet they live on."

"It is no favor to them," muttered Dr. Horkkk. "This death-in-life is an indecency! Their time is over. Let them rest."

Yes, let them rest, I say.

And so a billion years of greatness comes down to this: empty creatures rotting in crystal cages, while bustling robots thrive and multiply and eagerly serve. Our quest is over. We have found the High Ones, we have intruded on what should have been private, we have peered into the nightmare of the galaxy's loftiest race in extreme old age.

I wish we had never been allowed to see this.

I pray that Earth in its old age, a million or a billion years from now, will die the quick and clean death that planets as well as people deserve, and that no strangers will come spanning the stars to stare at the dismal, dilapidated, deathless heirs to all our magnificence.

.   .   .

We left this underworld of suspended lives and cheated deaths, and returned to the glowing surface of Mirt, and we thought our tour of wonders was at its end.

We were wrong, for Mirt had one amazement left for us, the one which has so enormously transformed the existence of every being in the galaxy and thrust us into a new and strange and exciting era.

Dihn Ruuu led us to a long vaulted room piled deep with the bewildering devices of the High Ones, and as we passed through it I noticed familiar objects on a shelf.

"Look," I said. "Commemorative plaques!"

Half a dozen of the bright metal disks were stacked there, identical to those that had been excavated so frequently in the ancient sites of the High Ones. None of the others showed much interest in what I had found; they sped onward to some kind of sculpture made of many thin spokes bent and bunched in curious patterns. But I called Dihn Ruuu over and asked the robot about the plaques. The robot scooped them up, spread them on one huge hand, and said, "They are activators."

"Activators of what?"

By way of answer he reached into the shelf and tugged forward a circular band of smooth white metal, pierced by three slots.

"The thought amplifier," Dihn Ruuu said. "Which permits communication between mind and mind."

"Can you show me how it works?"

"The activators must be inserted in the slots. Then one places the amplifier on the head—"

I snatched the disks and the band from Dihn Ruuu and with trembling fingers shoved the activators into place. Dihn Ruuu made no comment. At the far end of the hall, Dr. Schein turned, looked back at me, and called, "What are you doing, Tom?"

"Nothing," I said, and lifted the thought amplifier to my head.

I knew the risks were tremendous, but I refused to think about such things. All my life had been only a prologue to this moment, all the years of being incomplete, isolated, cut off. Now I saw a chance to become complete after all.

I brought the thought amplifier down until it encircled my temples.

I felt as though a spike had been hammered through my skull. I reeled; perhaps I fell; I could no longer see.

Tongues of fire danced in my brain. My mind fled from my body, roaming the long room at will—

Encountering another mind—

Contact!

A silent voice said—

—*Who's there? Who's calling?*

—*Tom Rice*, I replied.

—*But you're not a TP!*

—*Now I am.*

I knew that my mind was touching that of Davis, the *Pride of Space*'s TP man. I felt closer to this stranger than I had ever been to anyone. Our minds met and could have merged; and I let out such a whoop of excitement at my new power that Davis recoiled, stunned, in pain, and sealed his mind off from me. No matter. I was no longer aware of pain myself. I moved away from Davis' mind—outward—

Out into space.

How easy it was to leap across the light-years! In wonder and awe my mind roved the galaxy. I felt impulses of thought rising toward me here, there, bright glints of light lancing through the darkness as other TPs wondered who this stranger was. I touched the mind of Nachman Ben-Dov, the Israeli Buddhist, on Higby V. *Who's that?* he demanded. *What's your signal? Who are you?*

—*Tom Rice*, I told him.

—*But how—?*

I opened my mind and let him see how, and our minds touched, and I felt the strength of him, that rock-steady man. I sensed another mind near his, and probed, and it was that of Marge Hotchkiss; and somehow that unpleasant woman did not seem unpleasant now, for I saw beyond her irritability, her laziness, her selfishness, to the—well, call it the soul—beneath. From Marge I moved to the mind of Ron Santangelo, who greeted me in surprise and amazement, and then a whole chorus of TPs erupted, voices out of every corner of the universe, asking how it was that someone not born to the TP power was able to touch minds to them, and for one breathtaking moment I was in contact with thousands of TPs at once; I was plugged into the entire TP net.

And then I picked up the voice I had been waiting for.

—*Tom, how wonderful! I never thought this would happen!*

—*Neither did I, Lorie. Neither did I.*

My mind went forth fully to my sister, and hers to me, and the other TPs dropped away, enclosing us in a sphere of silence, leaving the two of us in undisturbed contact. We opened our minds to one another, and there came pouring out of Lorie across hundreds of light-years such a flood of love and warmth that I nearly had to break contact to keep from drowning in it; and then she moderated her output, and we adjusted frequencies as I was learning moment by moment to do, and our minds merged.

Merged. Totally.

In that instant of union we learned all that there was to learn from one another. She drew from me every detail that has gone onto these message cubes, everything from the boredom of the ultradrive voyage to Higby V through the finding of Dihn Ruuu to the moment when I had donned the thought amplifier. Lorie will not have to play the cubes; she knows the whole story of my adventures.

And I drew from her, in that first excited burst of contact, the essence of the paralyzed girl who is my sister, and I realized that I had never really known her before. It had been foolish of me to pity her and coddle her, to try to shield her from my own happinesses so she would suffer no envy. She is anything but pitiful, anything but envious. She is strong, perhaps the strongest person in the universe, and her paralysis means nothing to her, for she has friends everywhere and envies no one, least of all me. In the meeting of our minds I discovered that it was I, deprived of the TP power, who had been the real cripple. Lorie had pitied me even while I had pitied her, and her pity had been far more intense and with much better reason.

There was an end to pity now.

—*This is Jan*, I said, and transmitted an image.

—*She's beautiful, Tom. I know you'll be happy together. But why don't you give her the amplifier too?*

—*Yes. Yes, I will. Right—now—*

But I felt a fierce wrenching sensation, and my contact with Lorie broke, and I was alone, terribly alone, once more locked into my skull.

"He's coming out of it!" Dr. Schein's voice said. "He's all right!"

I opened my eyes. I lay sprawled on the cold stone floor of the long room. Everyone stood clustered anxiously about me. Saul had taken the amplifier from my head. Jan, frightened, clung to Pilazinool. I tried to get up, swayed dizzily, and made it on my second try.

"Give that to me!" I yelled, reaching for the amplifier.

Saul held it back. Dr. Schein said, "Tom, that thing can be dangerous! You don't know—"

"*You* don't know," I shouted, and lunged at Saul, who yielded the amplifier. I suppose I must have seemed like a madman to the others. They backed away, frightened. I gestured at Dihn Ruuu and ordered the robot to get me a second amplifier. The robot obeyed, inserting the activator plaques itself. "Here," I said to Jan. "Put it on your head!"

"No, Tom, please—I'm afraid—"

"PUT IT ON," I said, and she put it on before anyone could stop her, and I donned my own amplifier again and closed my eyes and felt hardly any pain at all as my mind broke free of my body, and I reached out, and there was Jan.

—*Hello*, I said.

—*Hello*, she replied, and our minds met and became one.

And that is how eleven archaeologists set out to dig up some broken old artifacts, and ended by changing the whole nature of human life. Not only human, either. The thought amplifiers work for *all* organic life-forms, and so for the first time aliens will enter the TP net. There are enough amplifiers on Mirt alone to supply the populations of a dozen worlds. Later, we can manufacture our own.

And so it is the end of secrecy and suspicion, of misunderstanding, of quarrels, of isolation, of flawed communication, of separation. As the amplifiers go into use, anyone will be able to contact anyone else, instantaneously, over a gulf of half the universe if need be, and achieve a full meeting of souls. What has been the special province of a few thousand TPs is now open to everyone, and nothing will ever be quite the same again.

.   .   .

We leave Mirt tomorrow. We may never come back; others may finish what we have begun here, while we go on to other sites. We can't pretend that we're doing anything but sightseeing now. For a month we've roamed this sphere of miracles, simply staring, making no systematic examination. We can't. There's too much here.

We need to go away, to take stock, to gain the long view of what we've already found, before we can push on with the job of penetrating the mysteries of the civilization of the Mirt Korp Ahm. Things have happened much too swiftly; we have to regain our balance.

This afternoon Jan and I will make a somber little pilgrimage. It was her idea. "We have to thank them," she said.

"How can we? They're beyond any kind of communication."

"Even so. We owe them so much, Tom."

"I say we ought to leave them in peace."

"Are you afraid to go down there?"

"Afraid? No."

"Then come with me. Because I'm going."

"I'll go too, then. After lunch?"

"After lunch, yes."

Jan will be here soon. We will go down into the depths of Mirt. She's right: we owe them so much. This sharing of minds, my new ability to reach out to Lorie . . . so much. One final visit, then, to bid farewell to the Mirt Korp Ahm, and try to thank them for what they have left to us. We'll stand before a crystal wall and peer at some incredibly ancient High One, lost in its dreams of an era of greatness, and we'll tell it that we're the new people, the ones now filling the universe they once owned, the busy little seekers. And I think we'll ask it to pray for us, if there's anything that High Ones ever prayed to, because I have a feeling we're going to make plenty of mistakes before we know how to handle these powers we've so strangely acquired.

       •   •   •

Jan is here now. Down to the High Ones we go.

End of cube. End of more than that: end of a whole era. We don our amplifiers. We touch minds. I sense the presence of Lorie and say hello to her. She responds warmly.

—*Stay in touch,* I say. *We'll show you something interesting, in a weird way. We'll show you the oldest living things in the universe. Our benefactors, but they'll never know it.*

Down we go to say good-bye to the Mirt Korp Ahm.